Books by P. M. Pasinetti
L'ira di Dio
Venetian Red
The Smile on the Face of the Lion
From the Academy Bridge
Suddenly Tomorrow

Suddenly Tomorrow

Suddenly Tomorrow

A Novel by
P. M. Pasinetti

Random House New York

Library of Congress Cataloging in Publication Data

Pasinetti, P M
  Suddenly tomorrow.

  Translation of Domani improvvisamente.
  I. Title.
PZ4.P282Su3 [PQ4876.A85]   853'.9'14   72–8389
ISBN 0–394–47552–6

Manufactured in the United States of America

First Edition

to Rae Richardson

Suddenly Tomorrow

I

Rodolfo Spada:*

Actually my name is Rodolfo Piglioli-Spada. Hyphenated.
In Great Britain, hyphenated names signify vintage families.
In our case the hyphen was added by my father, who, in fact,
had Anglomania. I could still detect it on his face, on his lips,
on his stiff mustache, when in '57 I went to say good-bye to
him, dead, to kiss his cold brow. I hadn't seen him in years.

I shortened my signature to Rodolfo Spada when I began,
relatively late in life, to write for the papers. I was the big
eyeopener of weekly journalism after the end of the postwar
period. My articles and columns made a fortune for the
publishing firm that employed me, raising it from a position
of imminent bankruptcy to soaring circulations. I haven't the
slightest doubt on that point. I never have the slightest doubt
about anything I say.

Now that the firm has been merged into the Group—one
of the usual mammoth industrial combines—thus giving up
individuality, intelligence and the joy of living, I have taken

---

*The sections attributed to Rodolfo Spada are parts of diaries and narra-
tives datable more or less between spring and fall of 1970. Along with
weapons, alleged drugs, etc., they were probably confiscated during the
search of Spada's residence at Brusò but later rescued by his devoted
disciple, the Venetian journalist Diego Boldrin.

secret refuge in the Venetian region, of which I know very little, at Brusò (I believe we are in the province of Padua) for the purpose of preserving my own mind with its particular ideas and visions.

I occupy two rooms in a medium-sized and much-neglected villa with a rusty Palladian façade, far inland among poplars. It belongs to my friend Angelantonio Fornasier, a big industrialist and a genius, who must have forgotten that he owned it. I reminded him, and he said, "Are you sure? All right, then, go—go there." I don't pay rent and I eat well on very little. Considering my minimal expenditures, with the money I have I could stay in hiding for ten or twelve years. Only Fornasier and his son know I am here.

I have no patience with nature descriptions, which I find useless. Speaking practically: if they should hound me and compel me to further flight, there is a fishing and hunting preserve not too far from here, with an isolated lodge at the center of a wide expanse of water where I could find further safety, even many weapons. It is all Fornasier property—a kind of enormous pond whose farthest horizon is formed by a thin, misty Byzantine line of houses and clock towers which turns out to be the city of Venice. To reach the hunting lodge I would first walk for an hour or so across fields. Then, standing, with crossed oars, I would row over deserted waters, using a two-thousand-year-old technique which I, an all-round athlete, would master immediately. All of this would cost me no effort at all: I am small, lean, tight as if held together by steel wire.

Somewhat similar to the early settlers of these lagoons, refugees from Attila's invasion fifteen centuries or so ago, I too am a refugee from aggression. In my case, the invaded area is the publishing house whose true center I had been. Aggressions of that type are now the most characteristic

4

events in the Western world, and, I believe, also in Oriental countries like Japan. I haven't the slightest doubt. The typical sequence of events is well known: the men and women in some business concern are working well, each with his own recognizable face, his own words and habits, and at some point, after nasty premonitory signs, there it goes, the whole concern is swallowed up, phagocytized, in one lump, blindly, by a new group. International capital, from this and the opposite side of the ocean. *Restructuring.* There appeared in all of the business and editorial offices of our periodicals the questionnaires to be filled out, the mimeographed orders, the perforated cards, the memos. In one word: violence. Shortly after that, I escaped.

As an introductory measure, I have decided to devote long hours to sleep. I have been here six days and I have slept an average of nine and a quarter hours per night. Utter calm spreads over land and water, interrupted only by minimal acts of violence: little funeral ceremonies for inevitably crushed insects, and an occasional kick at the dogs who come forward and start licking you: that's all.

Instead of improving the existing periodicals and holding on firmly to writers of my caliber, the Group, as one could predict, feverishly applied themselves to long and wholly meaningless organizational debates. No one was writing anything any more. The papers were compiled by obscure secretaries from clippings and articles bought ready-made by the Group on the cultural market and teletyped into the editorial offices. There no longer was any substance, there was only organization, besides the planning of new bilingual periodicals (Italian and English, needless to say) like *Mary Jane* and *The Mediterranean Tourist.*

At the center of all this we find a young man of thirty-three —born, that is, in 1937—the Group's man in Italy, B. G.

Crocetti Vidal. No hyphen. At first I thought his second surname was Venetian, but B.G. says it's Swiss. At any rate, Crocetti Vidal is a product of the industry of ideas and of electronic culture. His smile opens up and then stands still on his face, shining with executive cordiality and very beautiful teeth.

I asked him one day what his initials stood for.

"For Benito Giuseppe. I was born in the spring of 1937."

"What day?"

"April eighteenth. I'm Aries."

"You just grazed it; but you're right: third to the last day of Aries. Astrology used to be a hobby of mine."

"What are you, Spada?" He smiled.

"Taurus. Bull." We stared at each other a long while in silence. "Full bull. May fifth. Right in the middle. Also Napoleon's death, of course."

The more substantial part of our conversation ended there. Crocetti Vidal started talking about the Group's activities, using words like *options, projections, relevancy, integrative, priorities.* Now from his office as executive secretary-general he sends out incessant and useless memos, initialed BGCV.

I raised my voice: "Watch out, Crocetti Vidal. Sharp turns ahead. And be sure you don't tread on my balls. I came into the firm a bit late and somewhat tangentially, but as of now, I am at the center of things, the very heart of the artichoke, *if you don't mind.*"

I resumed in a more balanced tone: "I'm giving you friendly advice. And besides, you know what? You, Crocetti Vidal, are many people together, all of them perfectly alike. In other words, you don't have an individual existence. I see you everywhere, eyes, glasses, lips, smile, teeth, gestures, voice. When you and I were first introduced, I told myself, 'I've seen that young man many times before.'" I sincerely wanted to discuss this phenomenon with him. But he didn't say anything. I concluded, "At any rate, all of you Crocetti Vidals should take a serious look inside your own heads."

He threw a glance at me, luminous, dilated, but absent, and started talking about "integrated priorities" and "qualifying options" and about the Group's interests in the hotel business, on the Ionian seacoast. Nevertheless, I told him, a glossy new magazine to be called *The Mediterranean Tourist* was a shot in the dark.

"Thank you, Spada," he said cheerfully, dismissing me with a look. "On these various subjects, do write us a letter."

Human reality falls apart. So, only unreal people are happy.

I know a lot about hallucinogenic drugs but I don't even try them. The fact is, I am perfectly satisfied with alcohol. Alcohol to me means wine and whiskey. I know a bit about wines, their nobility, vintage, and I am one of the few in southern Europe that has a real competence about Scotch whiskies, but that's not the point. I have achieved perfection in *dosing:* how much is needed of a given wine or whiskey to obtain the results I want. I always have a vase with flowers on my table. When these flowers achieve perfect focus, an intense evidence, dazzling yet supremely calm, I know I've got it.

Then I turn my mind's eye on the world and on the future. The firm has no use for me any more? That's their problem. Meanwhile my mind is moving toward such a refinement that anything, some day, will suddenly be possible. Actually, in order to achieve that degree of sharpness you must first have given up all trivia: buffet dinners in wealthy homes of exalted cultural prestige, executive committees, important funerals, board meetings, cocktail parties.

. . .

The first day that I was here at Brusò, a sturdy little fellow turned up, about fourteen or fifteen, with a cubic head, serious yet always happy, practical-looking, with pockets full of pen-knives. I asked, "And who could you possibly be?"

"Vittorino Fornasier."

"So? What are you then in relation to the owner of this house?"

"He's my father."

"But your father is hardly ever around. Who's taking care of you?"

"When Father is away on business I fix myself a little steak or perhaps we all cook and eat together."

"All who?"

"Friends."

He has a deep rustic voice; through his large vocal cords he often sighs but with no sadness. Now he makes purchases for me and keeps me in touch with the outside world. I wish I had a boy like that in addition to Genzianella, my beloved daughter, so similar to Laura, her mother, though twice as tall.

Her golden hair waving in the wind
A fair young lady galloped on the field.

These well-known lines from Tasso's *Jerusalem Delivered* came spontaneously to my lips when I first saw Laura, over twenty years ago, at a horse show. Exhilarated, I asked who she was. Laura Horst, I was told. Family from the Alpine region. I had visions of high and wide emerald-green pastures, and of trees with apples that resembled her. I immediately wanted her to marry me. As a boy I had been very handsome and had planned a life without marriage, entirely organized around love affairs. I wrote my dissertation at Pisa on the Duchess of Albany. I lived among such characters with the greatest ease.

With Laura, in our early days as lovers and as a married couple, everything—her round face, the grapes we ate avidly, the car's plump leather seats—transformed itself wholly into love sensations. A healthy vegetative life, perfect for that age. Then physically and intellectually, I ripened at a pace above average; she stood still—never withering, nor, on the other hand, looking artificially preserved like frozen food; rather, serene, immutable. Even pain seems to pass smoothly over her without leaving any visible mark. When her sister Genziana committed suicide in the pinewood near our house at Succaso, I thought Laura would avoid the place from then on; on the contrary, she started going there more often than ever, bringing her girl friends, who are generally very different from her. Her very best friends have long and complicated clinical histories. Among these women all cut up by surgery, sensitive, receptive, she has remained her immutable self—a spotless apple, very healthy, her eyes the color of lake water.

She happened to be with one of those friends, Matilde Apicetta, when I made my irrevocable decision to escape into liberating exile, somewhat in the manner of old Tolstoy. The Apicetta lady was for many years in the teaching profession, achieving at a still young age the status of a school principal. She and I have hardly ever spoken to each other, though frequently exchanging very intense looks. I'm convinced my very dark and piercing eyes disturbed her.

Matilde Apicetta was my wife's guest in our villa at Succaso. I was upstairs, in bed, with a slight bronchitis. I phased it out properly. And one evening with fully recovered strength I came downstairs and found the two women in the dining room having soup.

"Oh, we love these soups." Campbell. Golden Mushroom. The two ladies added an equal amount of sherry. They got drunk on soup. I let them get drunk, flare up. Meanwhile, I felt, my moment was approaching—the moment when action suddenly clicks, the self-chosen hour, the day that dawns with its forehead already marked: my acute and well-trained eye would recognize it immediately and give it life.

Laura kissed me, saying that I looked flourishing and that they would leave in a few days to search for a place to spend their summer holidays. Every spring they arrange this trip, which can take them to the most scattered places, without any results as far as the summer holiday goes. Very well, I said. Laura announced that Matilde would first go for a couple of days to her mother's at Lecce, then they would meet in Rome and start on their trip. Very well, I repeated. Their business. I went upstairs, still feeling Apicetta's gaze stamped on my cheek until I got into my room where the flowers on the table welcomed me, in perfect focus. Shapes drawn with absolute precision, colors that seemed to bite the air.

There was an odor of lavender and of freshly laundered sheets; I abandoned all of this when the right moment flashed before me, at dawn; I took with me only a medium-sized valise. Clearly the two ladies didn't even hear the motor being started, the wheels pressing the gravel with a swishing noise, as of a dog's nails. The dog, as a matter of fact, howled, but it was late, too late to stop anything.

I experience, today, a feeling of confident calm. Every evening you can imagine a future event, and like the one seed, from among myriads of others, that germinates, one of these events, some morning, will suddenly spring to life.

For example:

Months or perhaps years from now, when the light on the flowers will shine, no longer occasionally but continuously, when my mind will be in a constant state of supreme clarity, then I, who was one of the great names of weekly journalism, will come out of my present confinement and find a position as a substitute teacher in some unfamiliar village of this Venetian province. I'm already attracted by names of villages like Maerano, Caerne, Piove d'Arsè—music to my ears. I will disappear forever from the world of unreal beings. Far from them and their businesses, my mind will continue to function, ever more acute, lucid, vigilant.

II

Matilde Apicetta:

Signora Laura Piglioli-Spada,
8, via Venanzio Predini, Roma

Lecce, April 21

Lauretta dear,

I found Mother much improved; we spent a whole evening reading nature poems by Pascoli where there are still so *many* things to rediscover! I arrived here the day before yesterday, the 19th, because the 18th was the birthday of B. G. Crocetti Vidal (to me, more endearingly, Peppino), who wanted me to stay on in Rome to celebrate. How could I deny him that? I have such tender and proud feelings toward him! He is *highly esteemed* by everybody, truly the Italian soul of the Group, the real center of the publishing house! Not to mention their clinical-touristic projects in the South! On the Ionian Sea!

Naturally I didn't fail to discuss with Crocetti Vidal the situation of poor dear Rodolfo. I told him about your ingenious idea of using Rodolfo's bronchitis as an excuse to call

Professor Dalle Noci to the house, letting dear Rodolfo believe he was an ear-and-throat specialist rather than a neurologist; I mentioned to Peppino the professor's advice to let Rodolfo abandon the house in secret, believing that no one would notice anything.

If that can alleviate his grief for feeling "out of the game" (Peppino Crocetti Vidal's words: "Spada is organically incapable of integrating into our new structures"), better let him rest, up there in Venetia. Angelantonio Fornasier, whom Peppino knows well because he is one of the Group's new stockholders, communicates that dear Rodolfo, in the house that Angelantonio lets him occupy, is spending a quiet life, in his peculiar state of mild delirium. He has made friends with Fornasier's son, Vittorino, a simple boy, *perhaps* subnormal, who thus unknowingly maintains a kind of liaison and will permit everyone to keep an eye on the dear sick man, from the distance.

He is precious to us, ever more precious. He couldn't face living in Rome any longer, poor soul, and he would shut himself up in his room upstairs at Succaso, writing his increasingly unpublishable articles. I miss the ticking of his typewriter. We love him. He would come down and look at me absently, lost, as though he didn't recognize me. Why can an exchange of looks between people be so absurdly important?

I also want to talk to Angelantonio, who as a stockholder can perhaps exercise some pressure in order to get our dear one a little help, some pension, which may give him back a little of his lost confidence in himself. We must reconstruct his fractured identity!

For that matter, Peppino Crocetti Vidal himself, who under his youthful efficiency and vigor conceals deep charitableness, a very delicate soul, will let some time pass and then get in touch with Rodolfo to offer him some work and make him feel he is not forgotten. I have encouraged Peppino to do that. A good idea, don't you think?

Let us postpone any other question or decision about Rodolfo—neurological consultations, therapies, clinics. There are many degrees and nuances in the wide spectrum of neurological cures and of the institutions for psychic therapy; some of them are like very quiet and comfortable hotels. We shall take advantage of our imminent tour in order to visit and consider some of them.

So I shall be in Rome on Wednesday next week, the 29th. And on Thursday we shall entrust Genzianella to your brother-in-law (how hard it is to remember that Camillo and Rodolfo are brothers! And yet, one esteems Camillo, while one loves Rodolfo!), and then you and I will be ready to leave on our spring peregrinations. In the meantime, affectionate thoughts from

yours ever

Matilde

III

Rodolfo Spada:

I've made a discovery about this boy Vittorino Fornasier
which fills me with cheerfulness: he has flunked out of school
completely. He did so last year, and now, even before the
close of the school year, they've guaranteed that he will
surely flunk out again. Cheerfulness, and nostalgia—the
same thing happened to me when I was his age, fourteen.
He'll be fifteen on June 24. Third day of Cancer.

I'll never forget the spring of my assured failure, that
melancholy joy, that strong and solitary delight. They would
tell me, "You'll flunk out anyway, nobody is concerned
about you, go out to the country, do what you please, you're
free." And I would stare at them with my piercing dark eyes.
It was my good luck.

I later managed to arrange a regular course of study for
myself, all the way up to my university degree, but always
in the spirit of an independent runner. In isolation, I acquired a solid cultural background which later paid off in my
journalistic work, and which will come in very handy now
in instructing Vittorino.

I told him, "Let's accept the challenge. I'll coach you in
all subjects and you'll take your exams as an outside student." And then—well, I said it to him clearly, "I wish I'd

---

15

had a son like you. Instead, I have only Genzianella, who looks like her mother, only double in height. Mind you, I love her very much."

"Double? How is she to look at, double like that? Is she beautiful?"

"Very much so, really. And come to think of it, she's the right age for you. Now she's in Rome, but in a short while her mother will be leaving with a friend, and then Genzianella will go back to Succaso under the protection of her uncle, which means my brother Camillo, and Adele, his wife. That will be the moment to go to Succaso some night, and kidnap my daughter. How do you like the idea?"

"Very much."

Vittorino is my ally, I can depend on him. He would protect my privacy with weapon in hand, considering all the knives he carries around with him. Besides, he stays at the hunting lodge a lot, and its very function is to contain arms.

The boy is shrewd and imaginative, I have evidence of that. There was an odd and threatening phone call at the lodge. Looking back, I realize that this call from Crocetti Vidal doesn't surprise me. No wonder he discovered my whereabouts: the Crocetti Vidals are born investigators, great collectors of abstract data, assemblers of useless index cards. The phone call might have irritated me: *it seems they suggested that I do some work for the Group.*

But I keep absolutely calm. Nothing can irritate me any more, not even this screwy suggestion. I have achieved complete nervous relaxation.

Vittorino, of course, reduced Crocetti Vidal's location data to harmlessness by answering, "Professor Spada isn't here any more. Ah, you'd like to know where he is? Don't ask me."

"Bravo," I praised him. "Always answer like that. Give

them false data if necessary, cross up the tracks. Give them names of localities either nonexistent or at any rate far out of reach. And if they should come in person to look for me, give me a signal and I'll hide myself in a hunting *botte,* in the midst of wide waters, and from there conduct our defense action, armed if necessary."

At any rate. You never can tell. I went to have a look at the hunting preserve, to study the lodge, the general setup, the armaments. Things have gone far beyond my expectations. General situation: excellent. I have new alliances. Vittorino's friends. Young people of the very first order, all in perfect accord with me, not as tools, but by their free choice.

The march across the fields, Vittorino and I—he with his knives all over, I with gun strapped across my back—was very agreeable and rapid. Spectacular moments of land and water landscape. To get an idea of these places the quickest way is to have a look at some paintings of the Venetian countryside showing upside-down trees in clear waters combed by a breeze, or a silver sky over flat sandbanks extending to the horizon. For the last stretch, by water, we used a small boat called a *sandolo,* and I should have liked to do everything myself, rowing with crossed oars, but to go faster we each took an oar, Vittorino in the back and I in front. Regular and intense rhythm; a smooth sliding over the waters.

We landed at the house, larger than I had expected, with solid walls and, naturally, many arms. Also a vast cellar. The proprietor, my friend Angelantonio Fornasier, an adventurous businessman and a genius, is an excellent drinker. I know all about Fornasier. I once made him the subject of one of my famous profiles. The house is almost always in Vittorino's care; he takes his friends there, boys and girls who must be multidecorated with failing grades at school. I understood them instantly, and they me. I fixed my attention on two or three of them, key people in whom my eye immediately detected original and trustworthy characteristics.

There is a boy with a long head, his mouth hard but always ready to break into laughter, eyes shrewd and flaming behind steel-rimmed glasses: a Latin American revolutionary priest. Full of humor, and passionate about biology. Looks about fifteen but doesn't say anything on the subject. Very tall, one and a half times Vittorino's size. His name is simply Luigi, and I don't ask for further bureaucratic identification. I feel he carries his "Luigi" as a *nom de guerre*.

Then the blond twin girls—golden, sunny, with breasts already budding, somewhat sturdy but quick, with beautiful open faces, pugilists' jaws and noses, but also a look at once sly and tender in their Adriatic Sea eyes. They are the Spadone twins. The name with the same root as mine is a clear sign of an almost magic connection. They all listen intently to me while I tell them about myself and my situation: "Vigilant hiding. Lyncean camouflage. A hounded animal, unseizable, with coal-dark eyes sparkling behind bushes."

"How beautiful," they say. "Does your daughter speak like that too?"

"Not always, but we'll bring her here and she will reach new perfections."

There is also an older man, thickset but agile, with sky-blue eyes: Vittorino thirty years from now. He introduced himself: "Achille Cedolin." His tone is very firm. He told me, "Professor, I could just sit and listen to you for hours," adding, as if by way of explanation, "I am a sailor." He nearly always carries a gun strapped across his back.

On top of the lodge there is an observation tower. Achille climbs up there a couple of times a day. He has a powerful telescope mounted on a tripod. With it they study the waters, the sandbanks, the birds, the fields, the stars. Every once in a while Achille points the telescope toward the horizon to catch the distant panorama of houses and clock towers, the skyline of Venice.

He sits on a painter's folding chair, puts his eye to the lens, moves the tube to cover the whole length of that faraway island, distinguishing, even through a mist, palaces, colors, Gothic windows. After completing his observation he gets up, offers his seat to Vittorino, telling him gravely, "It's sinking."

Vittorino sits in turn, presses his eye to the lens, observes Venice, then rises again and confirms in a technical tone, "Sinking, sinking."

Trifles; but they make me feel warm toward these people. Quietly satirical humor toward the Protectors and Saviors of Venice, who now constitute a world-wide club. A very influential member of this club, for example, is Daphne, a woman with whom I had a very intense love affair; she later slid more and more rapidly toward unreality, committees, fashionable ecology.

Present in spirit is also Vittorino's father, who actually comes here very rarely—my friend Angelantonio Fornasier. I got to know him in depth on the occasion of my profile interview.

My articles became more famous than the very people who were the subject matter. I put Fornasier in the spotlight; nobody knew him before. He had been away for years. Singapore. Tahiti. Brazil. In those countries he would build new hotels or renovate old ones, first raising them to the peak of success, then selling them quickly because he got bored with the place where he had bought or built them. This buying and selling of hotels is just one example of his many enterprises; he was active in very diverse areas. For instance, furs. Also organizing safaris, not in Africa as usual, but in Venezuela. I know all about Fornasier, but it would bore me to recapitulate here.

He understood me in a flash. After I had questioned him at length with my usual methods, minutely analyzing the working of his mind and of his imagination, he asked me as a pure formality whether I wanted him to acquire control of the firm that employed me and make me its president. I didn't even have to decline the offer; a smile was enough. He knew from the start that I certainly didn't want to waste time assuming abstract bureau-administrative functions, I, who was the center of the firm, but in a real sense of the word. How could I have done my work if I had wasted time on unreal trivia?

Now, under the Crocetti Vidal regime, there is only abstract organization but at that time it was different. Before I agreed to do a piece on somebody, they had to guarantee me a minimum of two weeks, and safe-conducts to see that person practically anywhere and at any time, whoever the person might be. See my celebrated profile of Cardinal Vianello. Or my classic investigation of the sense of sin among priests. In those days one could deal with religious problems, and with problems of humanity and conscience, all camouflaged today behind political brushwood.

Naturally, retired Ambassador Camillo Piglioli-Spada, my brother, though never having read a line of mine before or since, with his air of a big evasive cat, didn't miss the chance to utter his piece of nonsense: "I hear you're looking for trouble with the Church."

"Camillo, why don't you keep quiet? You're retired now."

"I warn you, uh, the Church, those are people who know a thing or two."

A superficial observer might detect similarities between my brother, himself an abstraction, and B. G. Crocetti Vidal; but actually the two, apart from the fact that my brother is twice B. G.'s age, are very different. I was thinking about that this morning.

The fact is that B. G. Crocetti Vidal, who at a first glance may appear to be made of the same substance and fiber as celery, on the contrary is full of animal juices rapidly circulating in him. His skin, closely observed, always looks a bit greasy; but it's clean grease, as of excellent leather. His main characteristics are intense vitaminization and perfect proteinization. I don't hesitate to formulate the hypothesis that someday he may suddenly come out of the unreality in which he now lives and operates. If that happens, it will be a consequence of my escape. I haven't the slightest doubt.

As for me, I had no choice but immediate escape, total dissociation from the Group, to preserve the essential, my own mind. This I did alone. Around Crocetti Vidal there were people increasingly tame and homogenized, ever more similar, even physically, to him. And life was no sea but a useless broth. Automatic reabsorption of any form of inventiveness.

At the editorial offices they saw me rarely; I was allowed to live at Succaso and work from there. I found Rome uncomfortable, what with its old tradition of maintaining no rapport between projects and actions. Sometimes, as in homeopathic medicine, I would try to arouse the proper antitoxins by injecting toxins of my own, intentional and correctly dosed. Or this is perhaps a better comparison: I did something similar to what a poet of my acquaintance and I had once planned in order to fight nationalisms and border bureaucracies; our plan was to produce and put into circulation hundreds of thousands of false passports of all countries, thus bringing about the collapse of the whole system. Never got anywhere.

In my case with Rome, same thing. In order to fight, by homeopathic means, unpunctuality and the general breakup of civilized relationships, I would make enormous numbers of phone calls from Succaso, giving and accepting all sorts of appointments and engagements *for the sole purpose of not keeping them.*

I didn't even scratch the surface of the system. The system, without making a single move, beat me completely. In other words, my attempts at disruption went totally unnoticed. I would not appear at the appointments, and in their turn, the persons I was supposed to meet didn't appear either. If sometime later on a brief visit in Rome I met one of these persons, nothing was mentioned, and that was that.

After my visit to the hunting lodge I returned here alone. Extraordinary enjoyment. When I came back to my room it was already dark. I put the light on and went to the window; in the cool and aromatic air of the evening, I saw the large shadow of my head projected on the poplars. Outsize, yet fully recognizable. There I was, immense within those trees; yet, unmistakably, that was my head, those were my ears. Though spread out into nature, I was in full possession of my single identity. Things are getting better every minute. It's almost incredible.

Swishing noises behind me. My young friends were coming into the room. Vittorino, the Spadone twins, Luigi, others. One of the twins announced, "We are here to cook dinner."

They set everything in motion; soon the large kitchen on the ground floor became a theater. "First of all," the other twin announced, "a beautiful risotto. I have the broth with me."

"I brought wine too," Vittorino said in his tone of such deep satisfaction that it can sound like profundity.

After the dinner with the young people, I had one of the most successful nights of sleep in my whole life. My splendid athletic training and my absolute control over my nerves permit me to achieve complete and very pleasurable muscular relaxation.

Today I am pervaded with a feeling of strength and repose. I see myself as a house, a structure with rooms and corridors; I proceed further into myself and find areas ever more profound and calm; everything is in order; feelings and thoughts move through me with ease, at a natural rhythm.

My young friends have reactivated other rooms in this long-neglected villa; they occupy them whenever they please; they make repairs, they paint walls; one room is being readied for my daughter, following our decision to go and kidnap her.

I have started to instruct them in practically all subjects. I have reactivated the crannies in my brain which contained definite traces of algebra. I have always remembered my Latin, and I speak more than one modern language well. Since childhood I've been told that I have a scientific mind. Today for the first time in my life I perceive my knowledge in its whole extent. I allow historical views their proper place.

I tell the young that history is not always right. The fact that a certain event has taken place doesn't exempt us from thinking that things might have gone differently. Phrases like "History is not made of *ifs* and *buts*" to me have always had a pernicious and obscurantist flavor. Following that line, you end up glorifying obvious imbeciles and evident ruffians. And simultaneously, you'll blunt all imagination.

I remember, during my last lugubrious period at the publishing house, how disconcerting some of my proposals were to the administrators. I would propose, for instance, press campaigns to urge the employment of young military draftees in contemplative and artistic pursuits; or to introduce into their programs the dramatization of historical episodes, mythicized with succinct and enlightening vivacity. While the office people would look at me like so many baboons, my young friends here get the idea immediately and burst into festive laughter; then they get to work on our various historical subjects, drafting lively heterogeneous "memos."

I'll pick two at random, one medieval and one modern.

Manente degli Uberti (Farinata), a Ghibelline from Florence, takes refuge in Siena, as Florence is in the hands of the enemy Guelph party. At the battle of Montaperti he beats the Florentines but opposes the idea of razing the city, theirs and his own, to the ground; so he becomes its savior. Twenty years after his death the Inquisitor, Salmone da Lucca, proclaims him a heretic; his bones are removed from his tomb; all of his children's and grandchildren's possessions are confiscated. In Hell, resurrected from a grave of fire, he again beats everybody by his stamina and dignity.

The Bellerophon *sails along the soft underbelly of England with Napoleon in front, arms crossed on his chest, being led to final captivity on St. Helena. Britons who for years have considered him the Devil and have thrown away lives and riches to do him in, now applaud him ecstatically, long rows of geese in agitation lined up on the seashore.*

It is entirely probable that B.G.C.V. may now be spreading rumors to the effect that it was he who threw me out of the firm. If so, he would miss, to his sole disadvantage, the lesson to be drawn from my historical decision to escape. Certainly my articles on the Church had nothing to do with it, whatever my brother might say. If anything, why not blame what I wrote about certain heads of state and government, men obfuscated and led astray by power, i.e., by a gradual progression toward unreality? Did my needling bother them? Was I a pain in the neck, an incubus? So what do they do? They circulate the rumor that I am mentally ill. Why not arrest me and put me on trial rather than mark me for the insane asylum? Really.

As soon as that doctor, Dalle Noci, was out of my room where I was lying in bed with bronchitis, I experienced one of my moments of supreme lucidity when even my hearing achieves supersonic levels; and I heard those voices in the corridor: "Schizophrenia. Clear as daylight."

Then I smiled. I had predicted that. I grasped the whole picture. Their technique was to pass me off as a madman; the same that happened to the poet Tasso and to other historical characters.

I pretended I sensed nothing. I reassured my wife, candidly: "By the way, Lauretta, thank you for getting me that doctor of yours. With these tablets he gave me, I'm already feeling much better. Good doctor, that. Oh, Lauretta, the new discoveries and the joys of pharmaceutics!"

Today around noon I thought rather at length about the positive charge—the power, if you wish—of what we are doing. With human minds collapsing all around, we make an attempt not only to preserve our own, but to keep it in free motion and sharpen it by imaginative and pleasurable means. The true, lasting rise to power. To the power of the mind.

Once a week I take a very good diuretic pill. For my

migraine, never frequent and now extremely rare, I have tablets which surprise me every time with their immediate effectiveness.

These young people and I take very agreeable walks together; some of them ride on horseback. We went to the sea. Sylvan, empty beaches. I tell them that Trojan Aeneas landed at some such beaches to make an immense nuisance of himself to the peaceful Italic people. I cannot describe how complete a pleasure I derived from my resumption of swimming, in the deserted, frigid sea. One muscle at a time, I recognized and reactivated them all, with a satisfaction that I dare describe as mutual: my muscles react to me, one by one.

Schizophrenia! As if one's mercurial ups and downs in mood, certain splits within ourselves, were not perfectly normal in anyone possessing a minimum of seriousness and conscientiousness, and discovering he's living among unreal beings! Our stubborn striving for clarity, for mental light, for the good, is considered fit for a mental hospital! Let us make a note of that. Cautiously. In silence.

IV

On the telephone, as he announces the time for his visit to his sister-in-law, Camillo Piglioli-Spada begins: "Adele and I will be there this morning at eleven-thirty, in order to make final arrangements for picking up Genzianella so that she may ride with Adele and me up to Succaso."

"We had already agreed on all that, Camillo."

"Well, but, anyway, I should say the number-one motivation for my visit is briefly to discuss Rodolfo, my brother, and also, in the very first place, your husband. Briefly. Do you agree, Maria Laura, on this order to be given the items on our agenda?"

"I agree, Camillo."

"Finally, last item. I wish we would discuss the little chapel near our villa at Succaso. I'd like to reactivate it." . . . "Maria Laura?" Continued silence. "An occupation for a retired employee, I'll grant you; but that's precisely what I am."

Laura hangs up, sighing toward Genzianella: "After all, Camillo and Adele's visits always confuse me a little, not to mention the boredom." She draws Genzianella to her. She puts her arm around the girl's waist. She presses her ear onto her shoulder.

The daughter speaks: "Uncle Camillo and Aunt Adele are very significant people. *Per se,* from their own angle, they are very flat people, in the pangs of death by boredom; but *to us,* without knowing it themselves, they are very, very significant."

"What *do* you mean?" Some of her daughter's talk manages to sound redundant and obscure at the same time.

"And then he's a bad driver."

"Pity you haven't a license. At sixteen, in America, you could have one."

"Yes, but I'm not in America. Uncle Camillo at the wheel is a menace. Then he's subject to fits of depression. Now he is a retired ambassador. I'd stay on in Rome rather than go up to Succaso with Uncle and Aunt. That is . . . perhaps . . . I don't know."

"What is it you don't know?"

Only once did the girl stay alone in the apartment in Rome, and there she spent golden hours in the arms of a beloved young man. She had covered herself with perfume and had worked long on her make-up, with final results that struck her as simply prodigious, in order to receive this twenty-year-old boy, Molisani, a soft-furred bear, by far the handsomest among her friends. She doesn't remember what he did to her; she remembers having told him several times, "I want to please you. I want to serve you." In the end Molisani seemed very worried. Had she expected more? Was their meeting a disappointment? She didn't feel sad or angry but only grateful to the world in general. "I am so prodigal, I have so much to give." What she remembers most distinctly is the young man lying on the sofa bed, tense and detached; she had settled him that way, placing a pillow behind his back and bringing him a drink; now she leaned over to kiss him, to search for his lips in the fur; and there was that interminable kiss, their mouths mutually upside down.

Uncle Camillo, seated in his usual armchair, crosses his legs; he has come alone.

He announces with a smile, "Adele is poorly."

"Is it true that she has cancer?"

The ambassador turns affably to his niece: "No, you irresponsible little fool. She has emphysema—quite, quite controllable. Nowadays most diseases are kept under control."

"You don't seem convinced. Does it matter much to you and to Aunt Adele whether you live or die?"

"I abstain from any further talk with you. Even when we go up to Succaso, between you and me there is going to be continuous silence."

"But I was really interested."

"Camillo, did you or did you not come here to talk about your brother? You had announced that as number one on the agenda."

"Right. What is Rodolfo doing?"

"He has put on this escape show, don't you remember?"

"Where did he escape to?"

"The name of the place is Brusò, if that can be of any interest to you. Up in Venetia."

"What is he doing up in Venetia? Father went there to fight in the war, the first one of course, but Rodolfo? Is he looking for silly stuff to write about in the papers?"

"He has abandoned the papers and everything; I thought you knew. And for that matter, Matilde says that he could no longer fit into the new—whatever they call it—structuring."

"Rodolfo's actions, whatever they may be, have never meant much to me."

"Dalle Noci has examined him. Although his condition isn't alarming yet, he ought to be treated. You know, one of those relaxation clinics."

"A lunatic asylum. He should have been shut up at birth. And mind you, I was ready to love my little brother."

"Love him how? And how much?"

His niece has caught him by surprise; he turns to her abruptly but doesn't answer, observing her in silence. Finally: "I find you prettier every time."

Before parting, she and Molisani had remained a long while with their mouths joined, inhaling and exhaling each other's breath, until she alarmed him by saying, "I wish we had lungs in common."

Uncle adds, "In fact, beautiful, I should say."

"That's because I make love very well."

Uncle produces something between a lament and a snort.

"Well, then, Camillo, what do you think we should do about this brother of yours?"

"Am I wrong, Maria Laura, or is he your husband as well? If I'm wrong, please correct me."

"Did you always have such a sense of humor, Uncle? Anyway, not as much as Father."

"Good; I really hoped you'd say that." To Laura: "Where do you think you want to put him?"

"Rodolfo? I thought this was what you came to talk about. We've heard about something up in Switzerland. Daphne's got accurate information, she's talked about it to Matilde and to me, except that Matilde has a good memory and I haven't. Like grand hotels. Nervous therapy. But I'm afraid they'd be too expensive for us."

"Am I wrong, or did this lady you mention, Daphne, once

have an affair with your husband?" . . . "All in all, I don't understand you. I'll never understand you really."

"Is that so, Camillo?"

"They already had hospitals of that kind in Germany before the war—the second one, this time—when I was consul in Berlin."

"Did they treat you there, Uncle Camillo?"

"No."

"Matilde knows a lot. Matilde is arriving today but before meeting me she is having lunch with Crocetti Vidal and Angelantonio Fornasier; she will talk to them about Rodolfo. We'll meet in the evening and we'll leave tomorrow."

"You are not going to South America like last time, are you?"

In the silence, the ambassador draws long solitary sighs.

"You have no idea of history. All you do is become intrigued with some fashionable guerrilla fighter."

V

In the cool, glistening conference room, around the shiny glass table, the meeting of the executive board is coming to an end and B. G. Crocetti Vidal is preparing to furnish conclusions: "What is being proposed to us, as I see it, is an escalation on the tourist front." He smiles, exposing impeccable teeth. "Whereas I would propose," he proposes, "a total reappraisal, without qualifications or exclusions; or even more clearly, the establishment of a self-renewing *condition of permanent reappraisal.*"

He raises his beautiful voice: "In other words, we must have the courage, or, in fact, the simple common sense to subject the entire structure to a multiple and continuously reactivated series of evaluations at the decisional level— analogous for each issue, but diversified according to intrinsic exigencies; integrated, but autonomous."

One of the board members, Angelantonio Fornasier, stares at him as if hypnotized, caressing his gaucho mustache. When he opens his mouth he reveals a vigorous, rustic Venetian accent: "I'd like to ask my good friend Peppino Crocetti Vidal to go back for a moment, please, to our starting point: the situation of what has been called our touristic-therapeutic structures. Peppino, I have recently visited the center we are building on the Ionian Sea and I've talked to Elio, your cousin, but now I wish that we, here, among ourselves—well, you see what I mean."

Crocetti Vidal smiles at him: "Thank you, Angelantonio." He joins his hands, presses his elbows on the table; he coughs. "I should like to open," he opens, "by establishing two points. First. The issue that my friend Fornasier refers to must be visualized, like all others, at a concrete, effectual level, properly integrated within the framework of a large industrial and cultural operation. Second. Each *single* operation must be subjected to reappraisal without ever neglecting its particular, qualifying elements—in fact, evidencing them."

"Elio was talking to me about a multiple-hotel complex, including not only the usual appendages like swimming pools, music festival, discothèque, literary prize, but also, well, a clinical area, especially for sexological therapies. On this I would like to . . ."

A young man with voice and teeth very much like Crocetti Vidal's, cuts in, "May I remind you, Fornasier, that our Report Number Six contains very, very precise data."

"Of course, of course, I'll read everything later on, thank you, Dr. Plinio," Fornasier mumbles rapidly, grasping with his robust suntanned hands the reports contained in plastic covers and shuffling them like playing cards. He has already tried to read them.

Another man resembling Crocetti Vidal, but in a dried-up, aged, graying version, cuts in, "We are spreading ourselves too thin."

Crocetti Vidal turns to him brusquely: "Thank you, Peritti. I have ordered a study of your statistical projections. I think Report Number Nine contains the pertinent data on the subject. But let me tell you, Peritti, and all of you, friends,

that neither our American colleagues nor I recognize a pro-
liferation crisis."

He smiles, his jaws relaxed, his tongue moving in the
darkness of his mouth, delicately caressing the palate, the
back of his teeth. Then he starts decidedly: "The essential
point is that there has been too much talk about a scaling of
our priorities as though there existed, so to speak, a hier-
archy in the degree of relevance of our commitments. As you
certainly have noticed, I am not in the least opposed to
openings of dialogue within the most differentiated thematic
range.

"But I want to make it very clear that in the same way as
none of us has, or wishes to attribute to himself, absolute
decisional powers, so there is bound to exist a univocal and
homogenized vision of our commitments and options. Ours
must be a well-articulated system of equalized priorities.
Frankly, that's where I see the straight path toward a fruitful
and incisive finalization of our organizational structures.

"In a sense, at a certain level, one might say that there do
not exist single qualifying options. Each has its own definite
place"—he smiles quickly and forcefully—"as in Dante's
Paradise. An ambiguous availability, a continuous setting up
of alternate hypotheses at the global level is worse than a
crime, it is an inconceivable error."

He tests with a deep breath the vigor of his lungs, presses
his fists on the table, not authoritarian but rather carried on
the crest of a strong wave of certainty and well-being; his
baritone is well modulated, harmonious: "To conclude, then,
we must continue to conduct our discourse along differentiated yet organic lines; there are several memos on this
subject." He distributes shining smiles all around, watching
everyone with green, affable eyes. "This is our line: to stimu-
late a selective, not a generic policy, at the same time leaving

intact both the structural quality of the whole and the mobility of its parts. Thank you all."

He rises; they all do the same and start moving rapidly in different directions, busily and automatically as if by remote control.

B. G. Crocetti Vidal takes Fornasier by the arm and gently maneuvers him to a corner. He talks into his ear while his eyes keep wandering around: "And how are you? All right? I'm so pleased." He holds him tight, filling with squeezes and caresses the empty intervals in his talk, his eyes always somewhere else: "Well, then. I'd like to ask you a favor. I must see . . . In other words, I'll be late. If you, meanwhile . . . You could go ahead. You and Matilde—right? Right?" He brightens up as though he were offering a juicy morsel: "The two of you can start eating, and I, later on . . ."

"Right, B. G., you'll join us later; Matilde and I will wait for you at the restaurant."

"That's it. Right? Right?" Fornasier is abruptly abandoned, Crocetti Vidal has grabbed the graying version of himself on its way out: "Listen, Peritti. Could you? Come with me a minute, Peritti. To my office. Right?"

Fornasier shouts, "Peppino, I'd like to talk to you for a moment about Rodolfo Spada."

At the other end of the room by now, Crocetti Vidal raises his index finger as a signal: "Very good. Bravo. You apologize for me to Matilde. Then we'll see, we'll talk. Right? Thaaank you."

Fornasier does not understand Crocetti Vidal in depth; hence he is dazzled by him. Every time he is in Rome, besides seeing Crocetti Vidal in person, he tries to get in touch with friends of his in order to talk about him. One of the friends is Cesarino Lugli, the most famous among psychoanalysts of recent vintage, a former schoolmate of Peppino's. Angelantonio Fornasier gathers information and the proper terminology to form a mental portrait of the young man and then work on it in solitude, retouch it, polish it in his mind:

The veritable New Man has given his life a truly modern orientation, whereas mine is the life of an adventurer grown old, and after all, summing it all up, I have had much less fun than people usually believe. B.G. has power over his fellow-men, he fixes everybody up. For instance, now he's fixing up Peritti, who was making objections, he'll cut him to pieces without the man's even realizing what's happening to him; fragments of Peritti will remain scattered on the wall-to-wall carpet with no traces of blood. Lugli and others say that Peppino is *an individual without complexes.* Fresh, healthy, handsome. At thirty-three, still a virgin. This condition doesn't seem either to disturb him or to carry him to mystical heights. Lugli, who knew him as a boy, drastically denies that he may be a homosexual. I ask him, and Lugli says, "Benito Giuseppe? Wholly different structure." Some of his friends are homosexuals but he doesn't seem conscious of the fact. Rodolfo Spada, who has the folly of true genius, says that B.G. is *not objectively demonstrable.* Diego Boldrin, a boy from Venice who works at the publishing house, says that B.G. is a case of *total lack of affective breath.* The excruciating sufferings of his mother, who died a couple of years ago of intestinal cancer, don't seem to have unbalanced him at all; in fact, he seems to have found them only bothersome.

Talking to Fornasier and therefore trying to use a clear terminology, fit for the semi-illiteracy of that uncouth Venetian, Professor C. Lugli has described B. G. Crocetti Vidal as a man *in splendid agreement with himself.* Touches of narcissism can be considered a useful safety valve, a vital outlet. Fornasier, eyes fixed in empty space, is thinking of that virginity and of that beautiful, virile, relaxed smile. Going to his lunch appointment with Matilde Apicetta, he repeatedly mumbles to himself, "High seas. Quiet, peaceful, but high seas."

VI

While waiting for Peppino Crocetti Vidal, Matilde feels pleasure and pride rather than impatience; she knows he is late because he is a very busy man. Peppino was her student in a provincial *liceo* during that sweet spring when she, though very young, was promoted to principal. Active, quick-minded, devoted, the Crocetti Vidal boy was the best in an unforgettable series of favorite pupils. Best also in the sense that he was the last. Later Matilde Apicetta was transferred to Rome on special assignments, and she is now secretary of a Committee for the Teaching of Modern Languages, whose members are high-ranking cultural figures, some from abroad. An important place on the committee is occupied by its youngest member, Crocetti Vidal, who, in Rome, has remained devoted to Matilde and has introduced her to key operators in the publishing and radio-television areas, and also to trustworthy doctors and to the right hospitals. For, indeed, Matilde has had several tumors, happily benign, and during her hospital periods she has felt surrounded by genuine tenderness and love. "Each of us has his own town, and then he has Rome." She also edits for a publisher a series on the history of women's liberation movements.

Angelantonio Fornasier, seated in front of her at the restaurant, staring at her with flame-yellow eyes, is saying, "No, believe me, Matilde, Rodolfo Spada is the most intelligent man I know, always has been; he speaks and writes like a god. I know, he did the article on me and he understood everything. Peppino handles words beautifully but in a different way. Peppino is an organizer, Rodolfo is a man of genius."

"According to Laura, he in turn considers you a genius. Except that you, Angelantonio, after all, have a good head on your shoulders, whereas Rodolfo, poor boy . . ."

Fornasier whispers, "You speak as though we all were your little pupils and I find this very, very exciting." He caresses his mustache; his eyes are humid, stupefied with well-being; he speaks euphorically, his voice rich with saliva, "No, I'm not a genius, I am an ignoramus with lively instincts," while his eyes continue to absorb the image of Matilde, especially between breast and pelvis, until his voice becomes choked, thus finding its right tone, entering into the same orbit as his warm, congested look: "Matilde, Matilde."

She stares at him intently and curiously with her olive-green eyes; she has an early-nineteenth-century face, neoclassic but not alabasterlike, in fact rather round and roseate, crowned with a vaguely Empire hairdo.

"Matilde, oh, there's only one thing I'd like from you. I'd like some day to have you lie down, beautiful, florid, soft, and I'd rape you. You wouldn't have to make a move, I'd do everything, Matilde. First I'd make you wet from head to foot with kisses, and then I'd rape you."

"How horrid."

"Horrid in what way?"

"In this little scene of yours, Angelantonio, in this adolescent dream, the most horrid thing, I should say, is the suppo-

sition of my passivity. And what adjectives—'florid,' 'soft.'
I don't see it."

Fornasier produces a vast, fatigued sigh: "Matilde, is it
true that you occasionally take drugs? And why didn't you
go on with that story about your great love? You had started
so well."

"I was merely exemplifying, Angelantonio, what Italy was
like at that time. I passed my final secondary-school exams
at sixteen, and this dear man I was telling you about sent me
a bouquet of orchids, accompanied by a blank card; everybody understood that it was from him, except Mother. Even
now she doesn't know. The other night at Lecce I was almost
going to tell her, after all these years."

"And this ancient love of yours—does he still live alone?"

"Yes, with maids paid by the hour, who always have
problems on account of having little daughters."

Fornasier doesn't clearly understand but he bursts out into
excessive laughter, then speaks reassuring, "I knew it—
you've never had an overwhelming erotic experience. Permit
me only one thing, that doesn't imply touching you or anything—permit me to talk to you, to describe and explain in
detail what *I* would do to you."

"I am not interested. I wouldn't listen to you and even if
I did listen, I wouldn't hear you."

"Well, then, why don't *you* talk to *me?* Tell me about
when you take drugs. I implore you, Matilde."

"I have only one body, my own, on which I have the right
and the possibility to conduct experiments; therefore I have
tried, a couple of times, certain drugs."

"You like to experiment on your own body, eh?"
Matilde shrugs.

"The idea of raping a former school principal puts me into
a paroxysm of lust."

"You are infantile. I suggest that you don't proceed along these lines. I am certain you'll end up feeling ashamed."

"A paroxysm of lust, Matilde."

"Soon what you're saying and proposing to me will make you blush."

"What do you think of Peppino Crocetti Vidal as a man?"

"Peppino too has his own childish sides but he is much younger than you are, and his energy and will power are not inferior to yours—I mean, yours at the time you were his age; besides, he can always draw on deep spiritual resources."

"Matilde, I was asking you about Peppino as a male."

"No woman can really have ideas on the subject, and you know that."

"Would you like to try? Move him? Agitate him? Shake him up? Exhaust him? Dissolve him? Destroy him?"

"I haven't thought about it, especially in the terms you suggest; but come to think of it—no, Angelantonio, I believe not."

"I knew this too. I still think you've never had a true experience and that's why you need a man different from Peppino, who has his spiritual resources—in fact, I once heard he was produced by artificial insemination and then brought up in a lab, in a kind of immense test tube."

"Far from the truth. His mother, who died of intestinal cancer, poor dear, was a young, beautiful and very sensual woman. Not to mention his father. A splendid boy. At eighteen he married this woman who was six or seven years older than he—a little bit, if you wish, like Shakespeare with Anne Hathaway. Except that Peppino's father was not a poet, he was an engineering student. He had the virile traits that were fashionable in Italy at the time, the twenties and thirties, and because of his perfect *physique du rôle,* he was inevitably compelled to incarnate that kind of character; they always gave him positions and titles in the youth organizations, evidently because his physique fit the uniforms so well. However, he was also a shrewd man, and at twenty, in '38, he left wife and son and went to America on a research fellowship. He let himself be caught there by the war, and there he is still, busy with plastic materials. Peppino, who has been in New York several times on business since he's become executive secretary-general, has met him and they have dined together very happily. I can just see them, seated face to face, resembling each other, with only nineteen years difference between them, brothers almost, there in New York eating their huge steaks."

Fornasier stares a long time at the woman, with ardor and perplexity; finally he can only say, "Peppino Crocetti Vidal is a fellow who enjoys his food."

VII

Ambassador Piglioli-Spada is reminiscing: "You know very well, Maria Laura, that when your sister Genziana drove her car full speed against the pine trees at Succaso and was found dead at the wheel, they brought her into the villa compound and laid her out there, in the little chapel; the poor woman looked like a statue on a sarcophagus. But with no sarcophagus! On the barren ground, since the little chapel, even then, was just that—barren, abandoned. Not to mention its present state. Rain pours into it. The roof is falling."

"That's exactly the way Rodolfo liked it. He would never agree to do any repair work, let alone reactivate it."

"But haven't you thought of having my dear departed brother declared legally incompetent? How is it, then, that his opinion even on an architectural detail—architectural with religious connections, by the way—seems now so important?"

His sister-in-law and his niece let these and other questions drop in silence. Then the ambassador draws his own conclusions: "It's all clear to me now: I haven't got any results from my visit to you. Chapel deserted and flooded, Rodolfo on the loose. Nothing done. Well, Adele and I will come and fetch this girl tomorrow morning at the appointed time, ten-thirty, to go up to Succaso. But that had already been decided. So, my mission here has been totally superfluous."

"Father says that all of your missions as a diplomat were toally superfluous too."

"I'm the first to admit that; in fact, I must have suggested the idea myself to my dear departed brother, but what has that to do with it?"

"That's the second time you've called him your dear departed brother. He isn't dead, you know."

VIII

After wiping the tomato sauce of his rigatoni off his lips, B.G. Crocetti Vidal is asking Matilde Apicetta, "Can you actually envisage his reinstatement?"

There is a pause; Fornasier is watching intently as though he expects gold to flow from Crocetti Vidal's mouth.

"Into our new organizational framework? Apart from his availability, do you really imagine he could integrate with our policies?"

Matilde, mildly: "You speak of Rodolfo as if he were a political faction to be considered for participation in a new government."

Now Fornasier laughs impetuously. With a pendular motion of his curly head he follows the dialogue as he would a tennis match between champions.

"Integrate with our new struc—"

"No, Peppino. I can't imagine that. And when I encouraged you to call him in that sad refuge in the Venetian marshes, and maybe get him to work for the Group, I made a mistake. I realize that now. I should have thought about it more deeply; and digging deep down within myself, I would have discovered certain feelings, certain truths, which I have acquired through long years of experience."

"What kind of experience?" asks Fornasier avidly.

Matilde rests a hand on his forearm. "There exist many forms of love, Angelantonio, and one of these, very important, very deep, is what I call clinical love. Don't sneer. I am alluding to the feeling of warmth, protection, love, with which a man can feel himself surrounded in a hospital or in any true, authentic place of suffering and recovery."

His laughter blocked, Fornasier now follows her with vague fear. Crocetti Vidal goes on chewing and swallowing.

"This form of love does exist, Angelantonio! I have known a great deal of it! And Rodolfo must have known it too, when they operated on his eye, or when he was taking care of Daphne in her sickness! He never told me anything about it. I know it from Laura. And from Daphne herself. Clinical love is something that Rodolfo now is in great need of!"

"Who is Daphne? And what kind of operation did Rodolfo have on his eye?"

"Daphne is a woman whom Rodolfo loved very much. Both Laura and I are old friends of hers; there is much comprehension, much affection. Oh, oh"—Matilde squeezes Fornasier's arm—"these types of human rapport, of human warmth, do exist. You ask what kind of operation Rodolfo had? A partial detachment of the retina, poor dear."

"But he sees well now, doesn't he?"

"He does, he does. Think, in his present condition, if on top of everything he also couldn't see."

Fornasier holds his mustache between two fingers and pulls on it as if he wanted to pluck it off. He murmurs several times, "Rodolfo is a genius."

Crocetti Vidal finishes sweeping off his plate of rigatoni, and while he is waiting for a beef stew, he starts talking: "First let me say this. A rescue operation in the case of Rodolfo Spada within the framework of our new organizational diagram, of our new Organigram, is unthinkable at the most elementary credibility level. But I tell you, with equal firmness, that Rodolfo Spada has had a precise and memorable function within our enterprises. This can be objectively evaluated."

"He did the article on me and I'm telling you, he is an absolute genius, he understands everything."

Crocetti Vidal proceeds without hearing: "Yet, perhaps on account of the very fact I mentioned, of the particular articulations of his past activity, Spada today is organically not placeable within any of our structures."

Now they have brought his stew and he is attacking it. Matilde watches him somewhat sadly. In spite of smiles, sighs, subdued clackings of the tongue which signal satisfaction, seeing him eat like that pains her. Having lived alone a great deal as a growing boy, with little money, careless mother, father emigrated to America, Peppino is after all one who has known hunger, and now, with a dark, visceral force, he firmly intends never to know it again. And all he eats turns into muscle, he is not fat, he only has that veil of grease over his skin which harmonizes with the shine on his glasses and teeth, and signifies a preference for rich foods.

Then, to lead him to happier grounds, she asks him about this morning's summit conference.

"You already know the basic themes, Matilde, the main lines of our organizational discourse." Crocetti Vidal proceeds, describing the firm as "a system of differentiated but homogenized priorities" and citing "our formula—harmonized pluralism," causing stupefaction on Fornasier's part and tenderness on Matilde's, for even in that use of language she sees the boy's conquest of affluence, his having been received, still very young, in the higher echelons of power.

Cautiously, Fornasier asks, "B.G., do you suppose you could let Rodolfo have a little pension?"

"The competent authority for a question in that area is Dr. Plinio." Everyone knows that Crocetti Vidal's own salary is not luxurious and that he is not at all interested in money. "Dr. Romeo Plinio," he completes. Then, by way of reply: "As regards the area in which I am competent I can tell you, Angelantonio, that Rodolfo Spada in our organizational picture has never occupied as much as an underdirectorial position, let alone a decisional one. I repeat that he was a stimulating presence but now he is out; his exclusion from our Organigram is like rejection in transplant surgery."

"And why, B.G.? Is it because he is schizophrenic?"

"Because he is tied to outmoded thought patterns." B.G.'s tone is clear, detached. Clinical analysis. In fact, Angelantonio observes, not only does B.G. speak of Rodolfo as if he were diseased, but he also seems to suggest that the man's disease—his inability to cope with the New Structures—is somehow his own fault, as with a boy who has caught gonorrhea. Except that in this case the disease is fatal. Deficiency of progressive hormones. Irremediable lack of up-to-date corpuscles in the blood. There is no appeal.

"One might say that the Spada case has been terminal from the beginning. How is he now?" But B.G. doesn't wait for an answer, he goes on: "I saw Benn. I talked with him for about twenty minutes. Josiah C. Benn. He represents American interests in the Group. He is also involved with very urgent Italian problems, like the saving of Venice. From New York he brought me greetings from Father. I reported to him on our recent selections of men at the managerial level, and I sketched our new Organigram for him. We have verified our complete agreement on all counts. The pattern of my thinking is always the same: homogeneity in differentiation; equalized values for diversified options. Along these basic directives, we have made the right choices also when it comes down to single collaborators, to individual men."

"What do you mean, B.G.?"

"I mean men who are out in front, Angelantonio, break-through men."

Fornasier lowers his head; he recognizes the new language. Once upon a time collaborators were chosen following pass-words like *efficiency, optimum performance,* or even *new structuring;* more recently, other expressions have made their appearance, such as *front line, provocative thinking,* or even *dissent patterns.* The chosen men have remained more or less the same. Thus, both sets of words are equally inacces-sible to Angelantonio.

Meanwhile Crocetti Vidal has ordered apple pie à la mode, simultaneously drinking a double espresso. Then he declares he is ready to go and rest. "You stay here and finish your *sambuca,*" he recommends. As he takes leave, Angelantonio and Matilde both get up. He embraces them both and plants juicy kisses on their cheeks. The proprietor of the restaurant and the headwaiter stand at either side of the door, bowing as he exits through it.

Now that Fornasier is alone with Matilde, he starts: "I don't know. I don't know. He keeps you and me here waiting for him, then he quits as soon as he's through eating. I grant you he's very busy, but he irritates me and there are moments when I'd like to tell him to go to hell, and yet in the end the prospect of not having him around any more, of not being able to listen to the way he talks, at least for the first few moments after he's gone—well, it gives me a feeling of empti-ness, Matilde, almost of anguish."

He sips *sambuca* meditatively for a long while, then bursts into violent, muscular laughter that shakes his whole big hard body. With his hands in the air he makes gestures as if trying to catch something, but finally he puts both hands on his head, grabbing his gray curly hair in his fists, and yells, "Well, maybe Peppino does talk nonsense occasionally, but he enchants me. He arouses feelings in me, Matilde. If I were a pederast in the original sense of the word, I think I'd like to make that boy . . . Hello, Ferro."

A man wearing padded overalls has sat down silently, unannounced, at their table.

"Do you know him, Matilde? Remigio Ferro, the film director. Professor Matilde Alpicetta."

"Apicetta, not Alpicetta."

"Apicetta."

"Hi, Matilde," Ferro says in a throaty whisper.

"So you know each other."

"How are you, Remigio?"

"Couldn't be worse, Matilde. I've blundered all along the line. But not just this time. I mean my whole life, the general strategy."

Fornasier observes affably, "I don't know why, Ferro, but your stories never interest me."

"You mean the stories in my pictures?" Ferro has a youthful face drawn with fatigue, round black eyes always moving, climbing the walls, searching. "I hoped I'd find you here still with Crocetti Vidal."

"No, Ferro, I didn't mean the stories in your pictures, I meant the personal stories you always have with the censors, with the courts, that kind of thing. I saw an article about you in the paper just last night."

"But wasn't Crocetti Vidal here with you?"

"He left minutes ago."

"In what way do you mean you've blundered all your life, Remigio?"

"Look, Matilde, if I tell you so, you must believe me. No use going into details. You are a woman of culture and you know that I, too, in the final analysis, started as a literary man. I was going to put all of myself in a novel but then I realized it had to be a motion picture. We talked about it once a couple of years ago, remember? Yes, you do remember. In fact, it can't have happened only once. God knows how many times you've heard me talk about it. I had nothing but that on my mind in those days. I spoke, thought, dreamed of nothing else. Twenty-four hours a day. You probably remember the title, too: *The Padua Dead.* I am from Padua, and I wanted to express all of my sorrow at the death of so many of my contemporaries. That's all. Nothing else. My survival; their death. I wanted to purify myself, I already saw myself with a Tolstoy-type biography, with periods before and after the conversion. And don't believe they didn't listen to me."

Now Fornasier is trapped too; he listens intently.

"And how. They listened to me with a lot of understanding. Some producers, as a matter of fact, would throw me out of their offices, yelling at me, 'I produce films, not funerals,' but there are also some of them who are very sophisticated, with university degrees, excellent people. But they also thought that I intended *The Padua Dead* as a war picture, dead on the battlefield or at the very least political persecution, death sentences, shootings —in other words the historical background. 'No!' I yelled. 'Death seen as an absolute, without knowing who has signed the decree. Persecution as an end in itself. The victim *sub specie aeternitatis.* A picture in black and white, or even more precisely, black and gray. This austere, supreme homage to my dead comrades. There are also those who died of cancer! Don't you ever go into a hospital? I live in hospitals!' Nothing doing. 'But, Remigio, with a film like that I'll lose money to my last lira,' et cetera et cetera, usual accursed arguments."

"I understand you very well, Remigio. Clinical love. I was just telling Angelantonio."

Remigio stares at her foggily and proceeds, "Well, then, I told myself, I'll make successful pictures. As of now I am being persecuted by the law, but I too, like so many others, have lived the exhilarating comedy of success. And how you pay for it! It intoxicates, but it's like cuttlebones, very very light, floating on a sea of sickness. For instance, I, now, *am always sick*. To begin with, my ears are buzzing incessantly, particularly the left one."

"But there are excellent ear specialists, Remigio."

"No, no. In a living being, everything is connected with everything else. In the case of my ear there are also circulatory problems, besides high blood pressure, and let's face it, elements of deafness. All males, for that matter, are at least slightly deaf, whereas females have very acute hearing. This is not true, but when you write scripts you get used to oversimplified truths. Journalism at its best is also that way. Long live clarity. Now, on the other hand, what with incriminations, censors, lawsuits, I am in a state of total and relentless confusion. Our latest picture cannot be shown, it has been sealed, blocked, as if it represented a source of contagion; they've placed a *cordon sanitaire* around it; this expression, by the way, was invented by Proust's father. And do you know what caused the trouble? No end of trouble? They've mobilized a number of parents who accuse us of having their little girls play scenes which are considered daring and immoral. Have those girls thus been launched on the path of sin? And even if this were demonstrable, would it have happened in reality or in scenic fiction? It seems that this time the case is more serious than usual and that the film director, which means myself, Remigio Ferro in person, may go to jail for several years. Meanwhile, however, if my nerves don't give in—but everything makes me feel that they will—this could be an extraordinarily interesting trial, on the theme of confusion between art and life, a happening-trial which would totally eclipse Pirandello's dramaturgy. But where is Crocetti Vidal?"

"He went to rest. Why do you want him?"

"He could do something, perhaps a lot. He has those papers, and then he has contacts with religious organizations, American ones too, which carry a lot of weight. I mentioned it to him and he answered me but I don't understand him when he talks. I tried several times over the phone, with a tape recorder hooked up to the phone so I could play back what he had been saying—no use. And it isn't as though he were trying to get away, to avoid you. On the contrary, he talks, he explains at great length, but to me it's a total blank. I'm afraid my oversimplified thought habits have caused a shrinking in the usable areas of my brain. Perhaps I am plunging not so much into folly as into the most banal idiocy."

His two listeners keep quiet, sighing. Ferro looks at each several times; his eyes grow tender; he begs: "Give me some advice. You seem so wise. Are you lovers? No? No. Pity. Wonderful couple."

Fornasier grabs his hand. "Listen, weren't you great friends with Rodolfo Spada?"

"There was a time when we used to meet every night, more or less; that was the time Rodolfo was going with Daphne —splendid woman, that."

"Who is Daphne? Matilde too was saying . . ."

"Daphne is of Welsh origin, I believe; she's had several

husbands, usually American, but also one who was more or less Italian. With Daphne, Rodolfo was repaying his wife for all of *her* infidelities."

"Now dear Rodolfo lives in a villa, up in the Venetian countryside, at Brusò; rather close, by the way, to Padua. It belongs to Angelantonio; why don't you go there too? I'm sure Angelantonio would be glad."

"Happy. In fact, I was going to suggest it."

The three of them stare at one another in silence, as if struck by some important revelation. Fornasier says, "Up to now, Ferro, your stories had never interested me, but this time—I don't know."

Ferro concludes, "I have the impression that an essential moment in my life is approaching, and that I must not let it pass."

IX

Journalists and photographers have often thought of interviewing Crocetti Vidal and of capturing his image. Interest around him has become livelier since his return from a trip to the United States, where he has finalized agreements with American exponents of the Group in the publishing and the cultural-touristic fields. The Group is planning to promote in Europe, on a large scale, a tourist movement toward America, where generally so far a trip to America has been conceived only in terms of business or of visits to relatives. Besides, cultural exchange is being planned no longer on the basis of single scholars or researchers but of entire schools and colleges. Exchanges in avant-garde scientific areas, like sexology, are also envisaged.

With all this, plans to interview Crocetti Vidal always fall by the wayside. Why? Perhaps because even in full daylight that young man possesses an innate capacity for hiding. He is present and very much alive, but as if camouflaged. And he has extraordinary mobility; a sort of sixth sense always enables him to find a taxicab even during rush hours. He has had long training in that, because all of his urban movements are performed by taxicab. He doesn't own a car, and for that matter, he cannot drive one. He comes out of his office or a restaurant, and in the overwhelming majority of cases he hits on a cab, ready for him. Cab drivers always greet him as if they recognize him, but they wouldn't be able to identify him.

That is what happened also after his lunch with Matilde Apicetta and Angelantonio Fornasier.

He came out of the restaurant at 1513 hours and found a taxicab after six or seven seconds. He could give the impression of being slightly abstracted in his thoughts, so much so that the driver, Ennio Vitello, an immigrant to Rome from the Molise region, asked him, "Where are we going, Doctor?"

Crocetti Vidal gave his home address. The taxi driver nodded reassuringly. Crocetti Vidal said, "Thank you," probably because he was grateful to the man for not requesting any further explanation, thus indicating that he was acquainted with the rather new street where Crocetti Vidal had rented from the owning company, on a three-year lease, an apartment in a marble-and-glass building of medium size and luxury.

Normally a taxicab ride from the section of town where the restaurant is to this apartment building takes between twenty and twenty-five minutes. In case of traffic congestion it may take up to a half-hour, three quarters, occasionally even a whole hour. This time the ride took less than twenty minutes—more exactly, eighteen minutes and forty-five seconds: a record for the month, perhaps for the year. Crocetti Vidal didn't appear to be either unaware or especially conscious of this fact. He looked neither impatient nor particularly relaxed. Judging by the expression in his eyes and face —at least, by what Ennio Vitello could see of it, reflected in the rear-view mirror—Crocetti Vidal looked neither worried nor cheerful, neither satisfied nor frustrated. His watch, a very thin and flat Patek Philippe, which he wears on top of his shirt cuff, indicated that from the moment he left the restaurant to the moment he introduced the Yale key into the lock on the door to his apartment (the elevator, manufactured in Milan, is of average speed), twenty minutes and a half had elapsed.

The condition of immaculate order existing in the apartment is to be credited to the maid, Pia Baglino, who comes in the morning after Crocetti Vidal has left, and leaves in the evening before he comes back. She received instructions of a general character the day she was employed. If there are specific instructions, she finds them typewritten on a sheet of paper, initialed BGCV. This circumstance, according to statements by Pia Baglino herself, who has an excellent memory, has occurred only twice in eight months.

Crocetti Vidal—again according to what the maid has confirmed—perspires copiously. He changes his shirt as often as three times a day. The same average goes for jockey pants and undershirts. Bed sheets and pajamas are changed twice a week. Pia Baglino washes the small things in the apartment and takes sheets and large bath towels to the laundry. On the days when she does that, her detour and her stopping at the laundry prolong by about twenty minutes her trip from Crocetti Vidal's apartment to her house, or from her house to the apartment. She lives in a poor suburb at the other end of town. To come to Crocetti Vidal's she uses a well-tested system of streetcars and buses. It usually takes her about three hours. She gets up at five-thirty, prepares *caffelatte* for her husband and her little girls, takes the girls to a nearby nuns' school to which Crocetti Vidal himself has had them accepted, finally arriving at the apartment at eight forty-five; according to testimony offered by Edvige Mescioni, the doorkeeper of the building, Crocetti Vidal leaves at eight thirty-five, without fail. Without fail because, at least since he has been living here, he hasn't been sick a single day. For that matter, according to statements from people who have known him longer, he has never been sick in his whole life.

Among the permanent instructions that Crocetti Vidal has given Pia Baglino are the ones concerning food. Every morning Crocetti Vidal finds a bottle of milk in the refrigerator, and on the gas stove the coffee machine (of the so-called Vesuvian type) all set so that all he has to do is light the gas with a match (of the "Swedish" variety, not *cerino* or "kitchen match"; a new box must be provided when the previous one is a few matches from the end) and prepare his morning potion, mixing the hot coffee with milk from the refrigerator to produce lukewarm *caffelatte,* tending toward the cold, which to Crocetti Vidal represents the perfect temperature. It is preceded by orange juice, also ready in the refrigerator; and it is accompanied by numerous pieces of toast (never fewer than four, and there have been high points of eight or nine), which he makes in a toaster of American origin. He drinks at least two large cups of *caffelatte* with a quantity of sugar which averages two and a half spoonfuls per cup. He alternates swallows of *caffelatte* with hunks of toast copiously buttered and spread with jam; both jam and butter he finds in the refrigerator, the butter arranged in little curls and protected by a plastic cover.

Another instruction is: no lunch. Crocetti Vidal always eats lunch out, and in the majority of cases (approximately eighty or eighty-five percent) he uses his noon meals for meeting with friends and as opportunities to talk about current office topics, thus turning the occasions largely into "business lunches."

For his dinner, his instructions to Pia Baglino are that she should leave, in the refrigerator or in the oven, dishes already prepared, requiring only, and not always, a final touch before being ready to eat. For example, in the case of veal in tuna sauce, all he has to do is pull it out of the refrigerator. In the case of roast beef, veal roll, or *pasticcio di maccheroni,* all that is left to do is turn on the oven and follow the temperature-and-time instructions which the maid leaves for him marked in a special notebook. If he dines out (according to Pia Baglino, this happens at least fifty percent of the time) the instructions are that the next day she should take the food home, intact or nearly intact (there have been occasional midnight snacks) and dispose of it with her family. In spite of this, like many other people Pia Baglino does not have the impression that Crocetti Vidal is really and actively generous, but rather that the possession of objects and money is a matter of total indifference to him.

After entering the apartment and closing the door behind him, he lingered for an almost imperceptible moment in the hall, evidently to organize his ideas and plan the details of the period—somewhere between two and two and a half hours—devoted to his relaxation and siesta. After that very brief pause he went, at a moderate pace, into his study.

Crocetti Vidal's study is a room almost exactly square; two of the walls are covered with bookshelves; the third wall has two large windows, and along the fourth is a large couch with an oil painting of his mother hanging over it—a portrait which her family and friends have always considered a poor likeness of the dead lady.

The bookshelves are largely empty; a practiced eye would detect sufficient room for something between one thousand and fifteen hundred books; the volumes actually present are little more than fifty. The empty spaces bring more sharply into view the two large loudspeakers built into the shelves, at the right distance to achieve optimal stereophonic reception. The record player, of a new model like the speakers, lies open, naked, on a platform made of the same unpainted wood as the shelves, about twenty-three inches from the ground. On the shelf immediately above the record player are two piles of records, of almost identical height, formed of about one hundred records each; and a set of albums, about fifteen, arranged vertically like art books.

Crocetti Vidal picked without hesitation one of the albums, took out the records and put them on the player. He switched on the stereo but didn't set it in motion.

He went to his desk, which is light-colored, shiny, immaculate. Always lying on this desk are a paper holder containing sheets and index cards of different sizes and colors, and a portable typewriter, brand-new. Crocetti Vidal turned the typewriter roll to liberate a sheet on which an unfinished sentence was typed: *Each issue should be focalized within a wider context without thereby*

He tore the sheet into pieces through a series of neat and quick splittings into halves. Already on at least five or six previous occasions, the maid had found similar fragments in the wastepaper basket, all practically identical in size. People who know Crocetti Vidal more closely have often said that it isn't in the man's nature to prepare his speeches and read them from a written text; in fact, it has been conjectured that his oratorial strength may derive from that kind of ecstatic sensual fulfillment which he seems to experience as he listens to himself improvising.

He went to the bedroom, undressed rapidly and entered the bathroom stark naked. Pia Baglino and others have stated that the most beautiful view offered by the apartment is the one from the bathroom window. It overlooks a street with trees and is at the right height to frame tree branches rich with leaves. Crocetti Vidal opened the window; the fresh perfume of leaves moved by a breeze mingled with that of his soaps, *Balmain Monsieur* and *Arden for Men.*

He stood in the middle of the bathtub, leaning over slightly to turn the hot- and cold-water taps and obtain the right dosage, with a distinct tendency to the cold. He took a bar of soap in his hand and smelled it for a long while, then proceeded to soap his whole body. Having done this, he grabbed the hand shower in his right hand while with his left he turned the handle that changed the water from the faucet to the shower. He obtained the right water output, neither weak nor violent. He sprinkled himself diligently, raising his arms to spray his armpits, or holding his testicles in his cupped hand, meanwhile directing jets of water against his virile instrument, raising his thick muscular legs like an aquatic animal. He changed the water back from the shower to the faucet, placed the hand shower back on its socket, and with both hands free, he simultaneously turned off the two faucets.

He stood awhile longer in the bathtub, so placed as to receive the full benefit of the breeze filtered through the branches of the trees. He raised his arms to let that clean fresh air blow under his armpits, then again he took his testicles but instead of holding them in his cupped hand he shook them, he waved them, he allowed that whole seminal part of his body to bathe in the pure, translucent air.

He dried himself thoroughly and went back naked to the bedroom. From a drawer he picked a pair of nylon pajamas; on top of the pajamas he put a very light bathrobe, brightly colored. He went back to the study. From a serving cart he chose the bottle of mint-fernet, the only one that was more than half empty among bottles all practically full. From the lower shelf of the cart, filled with soda and tonic-water bottles, he took a bottle of soda.

He poured himself three fingers of mint-fernet into a large tall glass, adding three quarters of the contents of the soda bottle. Holding the glass in his hand, he went to the record player and pressed the button to let the first of the records fall on the turntable. He sat in an armchair, his head resting on the back. With eyes closed he raised the glass to his lips at the very moment when the walls of his study, acoustically excellent on account of the empty shelves, reverberated the first notes of the music, the overture to *Parsifal.*

X

Rodolfo Spada:

I said that my daughter Genzianella is the right age for Vittorino Fornasier. What I mean is: she is the right age to guide him, being one year older. She is sixteen. My daughter is sixteen—how agreeably perturbed with tenderness I feel as I say this. We conceived her in '53. My wife, already unfaithful by then (but I didn't know), after the suicide of her sister Genziana returned to my bed, being instinctively determined to have a child, preferably a daughter who might bear the same name as her dead sister. I grasped her plan immediately, I predisposed and foresaw its development with perfect lucidity.

Physically Genzianella is the spit and image of her mother, but in a filiform version, and besides being better-looking, she is more sensible and more interesting. In expressing admiration for her in her presence when we lived together, I sometimes could sound quite uncontrolled, but she would smile and it didn't seem to bother her.

From the very start, I never thought of the plan to kidnap my daughter, and to have her and Vittorino get together, as a mere hoax to be played on my brother. Far from it. Every motion in my life, every leap forward follows a pattern. Like a flat stone artfully thrown and bouncing ad infinitum on a smooth and shiny water surface, so I see transmitted from day to day this feeling that tomorrow something will happen —something which will have been prepared and foreseen by me and yet will explode suddenly at *its* right moment.

The movements, the tempos, are essentially always the same. Adequate contemplative preparation (brief in the case of the kidnaping plan) and then the action goes off of its own accord. Choice of the right moment, offered by circumstances which the situation signals suddenly, in a flash, after preparations which chiefly consist in listening to life in its organic development. The extreme sharpening of my mind tends exactly to that—to the perfect correspondence between what I foresee and what will happen, between my imaginative act and the act that will, at its chosen moment, occur. I've said this in a thousand ways and I haven't the slightest doubt.

In a practical sense, the right time for our Genzianella operation is during the absence of my wife, who has left with Matilde Apicetta. That is the time when my brother Camillo goes up to Succaso; one of the reasons for his intervention is to keep an eye on my daughter.

My brother is a kind of inferior version, lazy, boring, and with streaks of malevolence, of what my father used to be.

My father and I never got along and he never liked me. My person, my habits, everything was genuinely obnoxious to him. He would employ the most stupid words to describe me; let it suffice to recall that epithets like "vagabond" were still in use at the time. And his French. French flowers floating on the waters of his Anglomania:

"*Somme toute,* you've caused your mother's illness. And the way you dress. Your *mise* today is really the end. Fixing oneself up that way to go out in the afternoon. Remember that the true gentleman is a person who lives isolated in the country, on a minimal income, wearing corduroy jackets."

To irritate him I would yell, in the language of opera librettos, "Alas, I know! Oh, pray, Father, say no more!" Then I would calm down: "As usual, Father, you try to dress your failure in noble clothes."

Then he would demolish me: "If you know this to be an elementary truth, why do you repeat it so often?" But to himself: "Well, anyway, I've had *one* good son."

This good son, my brother, Camillo Piglioli-Spada, is infinitely older than I. He is fifteen years older. But he's always been infinitely older. For instance, he calls my wife not Laura but "Maria Laura." Due to his long sojourns in the Little Italies abroad, he is out of phase, he maintains customs that no one remembers any more. And he has that short nose and those round eyes, attentive but evasive; he speaks a lot but he never says anything. *Somme toute,* Father, he can get on my nerves even more than you used to.

However, Camillo offers also some comic aspects, hence possibilities for amusement; the fun can blunt the nervous irritation and even eliminate it.

I believe that I, in turn, have always been even more obnoxious to him than I was to my father. Recently, after he left the foreign service, thus becoming a retired ambassador, I would occasionally call him on the phone and open by saying, "Camillo? What are you doing? Are you retiring?"

A trifle; yet it would plague him. I would hear him turn to his wife, Adele, who sat there knitting, and mumble, "Rodolfo. The usual jackass."

"Are you retiring, Camillo?" Idiocies, if you wish, yet they make me laugh insanely.

At any rate, let me add, in passing, that Camillo as a man has always been absolute zero. He had a son, Amedeo, who practically at birth was chosen and marked for the same career as his father, but he died of multiple sclerosis at twenty. Not even this enormous revelation of sorrow managed to shake Camillo's mind and spirit. For that matter, he never occupied diplomatic posts of great dash or relevance. The ambassadorship to one of the more neglected countries in South America was the dessert of his career. Nevertheless, the fact remains that he did reside in many different countries; but what he saw of those countries, no one will ever know.

By sending us to Succaso to kidnap my daughter, life will undeniably, in its organic development, also be aware of the comic touches—Camillo's foolishness, and a kind of punitive quality in the situation. It's a little bit as though the secret code book had been stolen when he was an ambassador; except that he would have worried much more about the code book than he will about my daughter. But he will be equally meticulous in mobilizing adequate police and bureaucratic mechanisms. When my brother arrives in a new place he immediately gets in touch, just like that, a priori, with the highest government official, the *prefetto* of the particular province.

So I'll leave my young friends and associates for one day, except Vittorino, who will come with me; in fact, I'll be leaving these places for the first time since I came here as an exile. And for the first time I'll get the car out of the old and spacious carriage barn where it has been standing since then.

No warning to my daughter, except by telephone the moment we reach a village a few miles from Succaso; with me driving, we'll be there in four and a quarter hours at the most. As a matter of fact, even without considering the hordes of mythomaniac and criminal drivers who infest our highways, and limiting myself to the cream of true drivers,

I do not believe there is anyone in Italy who drives better than I do.

A time of contemplative waiting until the right moment strikes. Meanwhile, heaven knows why, an acquaintance of mine, the film director Remigio Ferro, has turned up here. He was sighted by Cedolin and the young people from the top of the tower: a possessed man from aboard a *sandolo* was yelling my name. Luigi got a gun from Cedolin and shot once in the air. The possessed man crouched on the boat's bottom. An unknown old man was attending to the rowing maneuvers with crossed oars. All of this was exactly reported to me by my friends later on. I explained why Ferro obviously had had to employ a boatman: that rowing technique, which I mastered immediately, requires ability besides strength; and Ferro possesses neither of the two.

He finally was allowed to land, on condition that the boatman would leave immediately. They warned the old man that if he should give anybody the vaguest hint about my presence here, they would sooner or later sink his boat. They got hold of Ferro and told him to keep quiet and not to move while Vittorino came to alert me. They gave him newspapers to read and a flask of wine.

A couple of hours later I found him sunk in an armchair, his eyes staring into the void, in a state of collapse. Right there, at the hunting lodge, I subjected him to a simple preliminary questioning in the young people's presence. I started inventively, to confuse him: "Ferro, I'll bet you anything it was my brother Camillo that sent you here." I knew perfectly well this couldn't be true.

He said, in anguish, "Your brother Camillo? Never seen him in my whole life. All I know about him I know from you."

I used a classic investigator's method: whatever the answer to your question you pretend you don't hear and shift the ground. "You are from Padua, aren't you?"

"Born and raised there."

"That's why you came to this part of the country. But why did you come precisely here to look for me?"

"Angelantonio sent me. He sends his greetings. Soon he'll be here too. Rodolfo! I'm Remigio, your friend! You remember our evenings in Rome? Daphne? Poor Vladonicic?" He moved forward as if to embrace me. As a matter of fact, we did embrace. "All right," I said. I turned to my young friends: "Let's go."

We brought Ferro to the villa without addressing a single word to him. During the walk through the fields he attempted appreciative remarks on the beauty of the landscape, but nobody paid any attention to him; so from then on he only kept panting, trying to follow us fast walkers. He behaved like a man under armed guard, morally manacled.

After we entered the house he exploded into violent laughter, which remained solitary in its folly. We sent him upstairs to clean up (with Luigi standing guard at the door of the room we had assigned him to), ordering him to come down after half an hour.

He appeared punctually and I placed a glass of wine in his hand; he immediately took several deep gulps. None of us took our eyes off him for a single moment. Again he had sunk in an armchair, his knees at the same level as his forehead. He drank more wine and looked around with humid eyes. "Boy, it's wonderful here," he tried.

His attempt fell flat. There was a very long silence. Ferro fell asleep. It was getting dark and I listened to myself telling my young friends, "Tomorrow, I believe, is the day we'll go to Succaso."

They didn't even answer. Not necessary. They had had the same feeling, in a flash.

Ferro suddenly shook himself, rose, and asked as if in a dream, "To Succaso to do what?"

"To kidnap my daughter."

"That's a magnificent idea."

I turned to Vittorino: "The safest thing will be to take Ferro along with us."

"But of course."

One of the Spadone twins declared, "You could leave him here with us, but—well, perhaps not, he'd better come along with you and work as a scarecrow, sort of."

Ferro tried to look captivatingly at her, and that gentle young girl shrugged her shoulders.

XI

"Here we are, at Succaso, and my bones very punctually signal the change of air. It's the left one this time."

"Leg?"

"What else, Adele? Leg, leg. Then there's the head too, of course, but that's under a different administration. Head? Now they refer to it as the psyche. Do you suppose that man Dalle Noci is any good?"

"He has a great reputation."

"Was it he who came here to examine poor Rodolfo, or am I wrong?"

"It was he."

"All in all, I don't want to be examined by anybody."

"And why should you, Camillo?"

"This feeling that grabs me, as though nothing were present, or if I were somewhere else. What do you want, child?"

Genzianella has appeared at the door, her back is leaning against the doorpost. "Nothing. I'm listening. I'm interested."

"I already warned you at the start that I'll exchange only the strictly indispensable number of words with you."

"When you feel you're somewhere else, Uncle, where do you feel you are?"

"I warned you, I'm not talking to you. Also because you young people don't know how to exchange talk. The things you say turn out to be, oddly enough, complicated and silly at the same time."

His niece comes near him and caresses his hair. "I'm asking very clear questions and it's you who don't want to answer them. Why don't you write down your memories? That's what Dalle Noci would suggest, I bet you."

"But I have no memories, my child."

"Don't you have any memories of Amedeo, poor boy?"

"What do you know about Amedeo? That was before you were born." He looks at her in astonishment, lost.

XII

Rodolfo Spada:

I resume after it's all done.

From a café at Tigna, Vittorino put in the call. My daughter came to the phone. Everything according to plan. My brother and my sister-in-law go to bed at sunset. Immediately Vittorino told her, "Hi, wait a minute," and handed the phone to me.

I cut in, avidly: "Is this you? My child? My absurd and disconcerting beauty? This is your father."

"I can hear you."

"We are seven miles from where you are. Don't say a word." I suggested we would go to her and take her away; she should wait for us near the little chapel. "The film director, Ferro, will meet you with the password: *Ferro*. A young friend and I will wait for you outside the gate."

Sometimes she speaks like her mother: "That would be amusing, I find." Except that her mother has a fashionable lisp and slips over her consonants, so she would have said something like "Dat be amuthing, I find," whereas my daughter's exact and distinct enunciation lifted my heart and made it oscillate quickly in a proud and exultant eruption of love.

And now she is here. She sleeps in the room above mine. She snores a little.

The tenderness of the night ride from Succaso up here. She was tired, dear child, and Vittorino had practically collapsed. I drove masterly, of course, while she held Vittorino, swollen with wine and sleep, in her arms the whole way. She kept asking me, "Who is this cherub?"

Ferro was in a state of catalepsy, though with eyes wide open and fixed on the two young people.

I am planning to follow my daughter's development, her thoughts, her affections. What joy. What vitality. How different from the rapport between my father and myself, between him and my girl friends!

With all this, as I resume notes on my family chronicles while the children are asleep, I would be unfair if I didn't fully clarify a central fact in my past: I mean the dignity, the style, the respectability that I always maintained in the enmity between my father and myself.

I was most particularly offended by some of his misogynous affectations, banal insults to human feelings, to human life. To make himself even more disagreeable, he adopted a phony Venetian-countryside manner of speaking which he said he had learned during the world conflict of 1915–1918 while being a soldier in this section of Italy: "All of them lasses, they're either stupid geese or dirty bitches, you know."

I can see his soft lips, the shrewd wink, as he was saying that. I detested him openly; I, who was all for women, chivalrous, ardent. Short as I was, women made me fly upward.

Then Laura came, and there I stopped for a long while. Then, Laura's first secret infidelities, interrupted for a few years when we conceived our daughter. But then finally, the big thing, the sensational affair, wide open, durable, publicized. Laura is exactly the same height as I; and she discovered this friend for herself, this Emanuele Vladonicic, a towering column of muscle with hair of wheat and the white eyes of the seaman. I heard of this big thing of Laura's and I looked at myself in the mirror; I saw a ridiculous jockey with tears in his eyes.

As a boy, when I was very handsome, I would make love to thin blondes with significant profiles, not so much Botticellian as Anglo-Saxon, unfailingly taller than I. Now I was paying for it. In the front row, with his bill made out long ago, *mon père*. And with his phony talk: "You who used to be the little rooster, ha ha, is it true what people say? Little rooster, is it true?"

He savored it as his own vindication and that's how he lost me. I didn't even answer him, nor was there any point in staging dramatic partings, door slammings. I even let him use the obvious French word to describe my situation as the betrayed husband. I never went to see him again alive.

But I did continue to look at myself in the mirror, to bring myself into focus. I realized that things wouldn't go on like that! One morning at the break of dawn I saw myself in perfect lucidity, without a veil of tears. I was all set for new openings and fulgurations.

One of these was my very intense love affair with Daphne; another one was discovering that Vladonicic, whom I met during a memorable summer in Rome, was a wretchedly unhappy man, with financial worries and a serious heart condition. He ended up by practically dying in my arms. Laura, meanwhile, was creating a perfect symmetry in affective values by tightening her friendship with Daphne.

Years later, in retrospect, the Vladonicic case and the Daphne case were not among the least sources of inspiration for my celebrated articles on matrimony in the after-postwar period, which prompted more than six hundred and fifty letters to me by female readers, and a dazzling rise in the paper's circulation.

That's where my film director acquaintance comes in, Remigio Ferro, our present guest under surveillance. It was he who told me, in the Roman summer, "I know that man Vladonicic; he has played bit parts and he was technical consultant for a picture of mine that took place mainly in a submarine." Calmly, I asked him where I could get in touch with the man. "He's here in Rome," Ferro said.

"I know he lives in Rome, but where is he now, in mid-August?"

"He's here, in Rome."

"I had thought he might be with Laura on some island like the Aeolians or the Canaries."

I, instead, was discovering all by myself the Roman dead season. In short: it's a time when each individual person has value. In that world seemingly deserted, neglected, dispersed, everything becomes meaningful, acquires intense relief. In nearly empty restaurants I spoke to those who have only themselves to live for, and so they discover the infinite and unequaled possibilities of their own individual persons. Laughing with surprise and irony, I would think of the distant beaches and mountains, of the fatigue of idle hours, of the heavy and vacuous time-filling occupations during holidays.

Among those sharply visible summer individuals, I met Vladonicic at the Pignolone restaurant. There was no need for Remigio Ferro to point him out to me. I just looked at him and already we were in mutually perfect focus. He told me sadly, "I had thought you might want to knife me." And he stared at me with his white eyes, in which I immediately read a resigned and definitive despair.

I sensed that his suffering must be partly attributed to

Laura, who was wandering by now on who knows what beaches or mountains. At that point I missed you very much, my daughter. In any case, I told Vladonicic, "Look, the three of us, you, my daughter, and myself, can set up house together. We are very different from one another, but we all have substantial resources of authenticity and imagination."

He understood me at once. "I wish I could," he said, "but by now my heart is too far gone, both morally and physically."

"Is there anything that can be done?" I asked, man to man.

"Not a thing." As is often the case with very big men, he had a thin voice, with additional softness from the accent of his region, Istria. Delicately, courteously, he assured me, "My heart is completely shot."

Not too long before, I had published a very remarkable profile of Professor Grotti, the most esteemed and original cardiologist of the period. I took Vladonicic to Grotti simply to have my predictions confirmed: unfortunately, I had immediately sensed that there was no hope. Then decisively I had my daughter come down from Succaso; and that enormous man from Istria took with her, a child already tall and thin, his last slow walks in the city. Then he was hospitalized. And I saw him die.

This was the time of my love affair with Daphne, so after I closed the eyes of that unfortunate sea giant I ran to her, who with tight embraces in absolute silence tried to make me clarify my complicated feelings of sorrow. Daphne . . .

> We have lived for years
> in the space of lo-o-ove
> oo-eh, oo-eh, oo-eh . . .

Yes, in point of fact, right after meeting Daphne, I had taken her to one of the big song festivals. They are the most prominent cultural events in Italy but she couldn't understand what I saw in them. I studied that expression of collective art for the weekly paper whose lucky star I was. Daphne immediately formulated sharp accusations against us. Stubbornly, she discussed the texts of those amorous songs, declaring them to be symptoms of the egocentric exhibitionism of the Italian male. She talked about them as if they had been written by me and my friends, and also intended by us as statements of our personal and long worked out opinions.

> Oo-eh, oo-eh, oo-eh . . .
> And now here I am weeping,
> Weeeeeping for you . . .
> Oo-eh, oo-eh, oo-eh . . .

"You Latins don't believe one single word of what you're saying," Daphne would inform us.

However, I didn't fight her head-on. In fact, I tried to go along with her, attracted as I was by her and feeling secure in the marvelous unity created by the very first exchange of glances between us, so that even hostile words didn't mean anything—surface ripples which didn't involve at all the ocean depths of our passionate attraction.

To my group of evening companions, Ferro among them, she would say, "You Latins are always coming up with this mee, mee, mee. You get together and each of you talks about himself without any contact with the others, always this mee, mee, mee. There is never any rapport between you."

I was extremely busy at the time, writing between one thousand and fifteen hundred words a day. As I said, I didn't antagonize Daphne. On the contrary: "Perhaps you're right about me and my friends. But after the intense manipulation of responsible words during long hours of the day, in the evening each of us goes on freewheeling without listening to himself. If you have nothing better to suggest . . ."

"What, for instance, would be better?"

The exact moment had struck: "Acting, thus liberating oneself from the network of voices. Looking at each other, squeezing each other, kissing without saying a word."

So we started our rapport, repeatedly achieving a state of amorous rapture and rediscovering the use of relevant and restful words.

I could even talk to her about little facts concerning myself, trifling misfortunes: "Once upon a time I used to ride on horseback, but then one day I had a bad fall, my head hit the ground and from the trauma I got a partial detachment of the retina. It can be cured through eye surgery. The worst of it is the period of total immobility, blindfolded and supine."

Instead of acting like the innumerable adolescents between thirteen and seventy, who, at this point, winking and giggling, would say to me, "You got hit on the head, ha ha, that's how you got to be the way you are," Daphne spoke with simplicity and competence. Among my wife's friends, she was the one who had had the most varied clinical experiences, both physical and psychological, and she treated the others with slight disdain.

Even Matilde Apicetta, she said, had, in spite of her tumors, never fully grasped the meaning of pain, and consequently that of joy; she possessed no organic sense of life. Mixing clinical themes with political views, Daphne went on, "Matilde has all the information about these political parties and trends, but she is always stuck in the same place; she has all the facts, but she stands still."

"You, on the contrary," I flattered her, caressing her body, her face, "are one of those who change every morning, a creature who can renew her vital juices continuously."

"The whole world is running out of vital juices," she retorted immediately. "A friend in the United States sent me some pictures. Look." A river aflame because of oil leaks. Sea gulls from the Pacific, covered with crude oil, clumsy, paralyzed by that black, dense, fetid glue, waiting to die of it. Mounds of fish, already dead in black gold. "They can save a few seals, brushing them, liberating the pores, but someday not a living thing, men, animals, birds, plants, nothing will be allowed to breathe any more."

Ferro interrupted me, coming to sit here. "I was watching your daughter sleep." As is the case with weak minds, he has been captured by telepathy in my thought wave: "While she sleeps so calmly, her entire body seems to breathe; watching her gives me a deep emotion. I know I'll never have the love of a woman like that, but even watching her means life, oxygen, to me."

For that matter, this last phrase has always been one of Ferro's favorites. The most varied things, a woman, a city, a medication, Genzianella, London, Parmedolin, represent for a while "life, oxygen" to him. He has a considerable gap between his front teeth, so he hisses when he speaks. He jumps without any warning from one subject to another, his head lowered, his eyes worriedly wandering. He presents his problems and then doesn't wait for answers. Reproducing him amuses me. I have a steel-trap memory; even when I wrote my profiles I never used any tape recorders.

"The jet set doesn't convince me. I've flown a lot and I know. Look at stewardesses. Pale, dark circles under their eyes, all sorts of complaints that haven't been fully evaluated yet by medical pathology. Jet life: champagne and a syrupy motion picture, and as reading material, along with magazines like *Esquire, Playboy, The New Yorker,* there's also the Bible, *Holy Bible,* and you would obviously expect it to be bound in psychedelic colors. Not at all: black as a priest."

But his fixed idea is his bad luck as an artist: "A man like me will never get recognition. But then the histories of arts and letters are all radically wrong from first to last. A panorama of mummies, a freezing of falsifications which have become dogma. Add to that the fact that by now even academic critics work almost exclusively on their contemporaries with whom they are tied by commercial interests."

He stops in midair. He always brings up subjects and then immediately forgets about them. Soap bubbles, they come out of his mouth, they fly around iridescent for a while, then blow up in silence.

He returns to my daughter: "She described to me the feelings she has when she holds Vittorino in her arms. Like squeezing a young bear but also like drinking wine from a big bottle. She kisses him tenderly also when he is sunk in sleep. Did you notice?"

Of course I keep silent.

"Your daughter to me is life, oxygen, she's always been that."

As I said already, these peremptory statements are typical of Ferro's neurosis.

He went back upstairs and I heard him playing games with one of the Spadone twins. Later I went up myself and found him lying on the bed, fully dressed, boots included. (He doesn't wear coat and pants but overalls.) Both Spadone twins, glowing, warm with wine, wearing bathrobes, were observing him. Rather than asleep, he seemed to be in a coma.

Suddenly he starts agitating his legs, beating the blanket with his heels, shouting "Damn . . ." and launching into a violent series of curses.

I ask him "What is it?"

"I had completely come out of myself. I was someone else. I saw myself from the outside. Now I'm coming back in, and I revolt against this imprisonment."

I understand him. I have had similar experiences but I've passed beyond them long ago.

He sits up on the bed, contracting his lips; in fact, his whole body is contracted, a knot of muscles, and he emits a guttural lament: "It's so funny it kills me." He adds "And yet it's worth the effort, you know, being a man and not a bovine. Keep telling this to your boys and girls here."

He rubs his eyes and looks around; in other words, he wakes up; he smiles coyly at me, he is tamed, ready for compromise; he has given up, at least for the time being, the struggle against bovinity.

I had come back downstairs and then my daughter came in wearing a long nightgown, rubbing her eyes with the back of her hand; she sat on my lap and for a long while we kissed each other. Suddenly she remembers something, gets up, goes out, comes back and stops near me, standing straight; she extends her long arm toward me and with her special smile hands me a letter. Oh, the invigorating loveliness of memories that come back alive: that gesture, that smile!

As a child she would act like that when she brought me the little pictures she had done. I have saved some of them: the usual circle, not round exactly, representing the sun, surrounded by crooked thorns representing the rays; and basking in that sun, golden animals drawn with surprising skill. I had one of them framed: a lion, extremely amiable, intelligent, affable; he is at Succaso, where he'll keep an eye on Camillo.

Later on, as an adolescent, she would hand to me in the same way pieces of paper with verse scribbled on them. I remember for instance:

> *All govverments the moddern age has had*
> *Have been awffully bad;*
> *Not to mention antiqquity:*
> *Obsennity and iniqquity.*

However, I believe they were suggested to her by her so-called intelligent friends; my daughter, if anything, must have added those double consonants; and for that matter she rather favored not the intelligent types, but the absent-minded and shy ones, like that young man Molisani, who, incidentally, is very handsome.

Now her gesture is as astonishingly graceful as ever, although she doesn't offer me either pictures or little verses; she hands me a letter which turns out to be a special delivery from Angelantonio Fornasier. Hot news: he announces the imminent arrival of Remigio Ferro, who has been here for quite a while already.

My daughter is back on my lap and I punctuate my rapid reading with kisses on her soft, warm cheek.

She speaks: "They didn't bring you the letter because they believe you're not interested in getting mail. I had gone down to eat a little piece of cheese and I saw the letter on the kitchen table. What is it? And why do you read it?"

"Well, as long as you brought it to me."

I also tell her what it's about, but she doesn't pay any attention. Her total indifference floods me with joy. So I go on speaking into empty space: "Fornasier writes that some of the employees in the firm plan to fight the Group. Apparently Boldrin is their leader. It's their business, of course."

Now my daughter surprises me: "Diego Boldrin is your creature. You taught him all he knows."

I kiss her once more without saying anything. In a way, she is right. Boldrin learned everything from me. Diego Boldrin. A boy from Venice, with an enormous head. Nevertheless, I cannot salvage that head for him, along with the mind it contains; he must personally attend to the salvaging, otherwise the whole operation would be plunged into unreality.

A voice rises behind me: "The spectacle of your love is ecstasy to me." Needless to say, it's Ferro. I tear up the letter and throw it away. I tell Ferro, "Fornasier writes to inform me that you'll soon be here among us." I stare at him with gravity. "Is this true? Do you also have evidence of that?"

In a state of mild hallucination, he asks "What do *you* think?" I don't say a word. Now he gets a bit panicky: "What else does Fornasier write? Does he write anything about Crocetti Vidal?"

"Weren't you listening behind my back?"

"No. I had lingered awhile to contemplate your love." I keep silent. He explains: "I was asking you about Crocetti Vidal because being connected with important religious groups, he could have helped me in my troubles with vigilante committees, censors, law-enforcement officials. They'll prosecute me in Italy, and then dozens of other countries will go on prosecuting me, endlessly. Ninety years old, stooped, toothless, deaf, I'll wander from place to place, from continent to continent, on my legal pilgrimage. I talked to Crocetti Vidal over the phone in Rome, and he gave me advice which I find incomprehensible. He said, 'Ferro, see that you punctuate and integrate your explicative elements, which may eventually become defensive elements.' And on a sentence like that he leaves you, with affectionate farewells, and hangs up. I remember everything verbatim because I've got him down on tape."

On the background of the Venetian countryside the already remote image of Crocetti Vidal is totally faded, but Ferro insists: "I don't know whether it's the same with you, but I know that for instance with Angelantonio Fornasier it works the way it does with me: I get hypnotized by Crocetti Vidal's talk."

After a long tender embrace my daughter disentangles herself from me, announcing that she is going back to sleep. First she'll go through the kitchen and eat another slice of cheese.

Ferro stares at us as if expecting some important revelation. After my daughter has gone and the two of us are alone, I hear his anxious panting against the silence-filled background of the Venetian marshes.

"That is a cheese they make around here," I reveal to Ferro. "Very cheap and really excellent. Accompanied by the local wine, it's practically insuperable."

He looks at me as though he were drowning. But he doesn't drown. All in all, life here is good for him.

XIII

The Group has requested five hundred copies of the Organigram; B. G. Crocetti Vidal, seated behind his desk, is casually leafing through the page proofs. The written word has no attraction for him. Even the memos and questionnaires which his secretaries uninterruptedly distribute through the various offices receive scant attention from him; he quickly initials them after members of his staff have gathered a general outline viva voce from him and have drafted the texts.

The Organigram is divided into two sections. The first part comprises a series of charts showing the personnel structure in the various divisions of the firm. Here the names are listed in a well-ordered pattern and linked by straight lines, ramified as in genealogical trees. The second part is an alphabetical index of those same names, each followed by short professional data. Crocetti Vidal has heard that the Group also possesses individual notes on each employee's political position; he could easily obtain that classified material, but it does not interest him.

Three people are now seated in front of him: Matilde Apicetta, Laura Piglioli-Spada, and between the two ladies, Angelantonio Fornasier.

Crocetti Vidal is saying, "No, Angelantonio."

"So. You confirm that. He's out."

"Our Venetian friend, Diego Boldrin, is not included in the Organigram; he's outside our permanent personnel structure."

Fornasier is at last confronted with a clear idea: Boldrin is the leader of dissent; hence, Boldrin is out.

But Crocetti Vidal proceeds "Our friend Boldrin doesn't possess the qualities and the image of the progressive avantgarde man. We are fond of him. But he does not have the stimulating, provocative mental openness, the capacity to break with outmoded thought patterns, which our operations require."

Fornasier is paralyzed.

Crocetti Vidal asks Matilde and Laura whether they would like coffee.

"Not for me, thank you, or rather, yes, but you'd have the coffee brought up from the café here below, so by the time it arrives here it would be tepid, that is to say, undrinkable, I find."

"No, Laura. They have their own espresso machine up here."

"Can you swear to that, Matilde?"

Crocetti Vidal is already transmitting the coffee order via intercom, and for the first time Laura observes him: she discovers that he has a very attractive mouth. Very young. No known feminine attachments. She imagines he must be a man given to hasty utilitarian sex with paid girls; this idea tickles her. Imagining those girls, she feels a vague sting of envy. Moments of total submission to a fleshy and probably very efficient man; and for the rest of the time, freedom, light-heartedness. She has known only one period of love, with Rodolfo before their marriage. Those months are to her like a navigation on a smooth and scintillating tropical sea, which sometimes reappears in her dreams. Afterward, she has only longed to be a serviceable girl, to be used as a convenience, quickly, with force. She has never really succeeded. All of her men—with Emanuele Vladonicic right up front, the tallest of them all—have always ended up in despair and lamentations. She has listened to them without interest. She looks now with a feeling of repose at Crocetti Vidal's mouth because his brisk and self-assured talk has always been totally incomprehensible to her.

They bring her blistering hot coffee and she drinks it in two gulps. While her eyes are fixed on Crocetti Vidal's mouth, she keeps her own lips hidden behind the cup, caressing the bottom with the tip of her tongue.

He taps the page proofs of the Organigram with two fingers: "This, basically, answers two structural questions: 'Who?' and 'Where?' Now we have to have answers to the question: 'When?' "

"What do you mean, Peppino?" from Matilde.

"My new proposal to the Group is the establishment of a Chronogram. The structure of our commitments and deadlines in daily, weekly, monthly and yearly dimensions. Our projections will be articulated on a triennial pattern."

"I find that you, Peppino, have a marvelous voice. I don't know how to put it. I have an idea that if Genzianella, my daughter, was here, she would say, 'That's a voice I'd like to drink.' That's the way she talks, you know? And I realize it has become my way too, a little bit, sometimes, perhaps. We imitate our daughters. In speech. In dress, too. Why not? Don't you find?" It all falls into silence.

Softly, Matilde fills the void: "How is Genzianella?"

"Very well, as usual. She's a person with such capacity for enjoyment, I would say. Pity that her father has decided to disappear, to vanish up there in Venetia, but then, she gets along with Camillo too, after all. But it's a different thing. And with Adele. Adele is poorly."

"Emphysema, isn't it?"

"That, and other things. But I'm sure Genzianella is perfectly happy up at Succaso, in spite of boredom; she has the power to find boredom amusing. Camillo and Adele are very pious, but not in a truly religious sense. I find that Rodolfo was right."

"You mean the little chapel?" With each of her questions Matilde casts a glance toward Crocetti Vidal to involve him, but in vain.

Laura observes, "You, Peppino, have also a beautiful *mouth.*"

Crocetti Vidal smiles, his head lowered.

"Don't tell me you don't know. Marvelous eyes, too. Green, I realize this very minute."

An evasive grunt from Crocetti Vidal. It is evident that he doesn't pay any attention to the two women. Laura shrugs. The man is a great source of energy but he just spins around in the void, so his powerful charge is wasted. She laughs in his face, fixing her icy eyes on him: "I've heard that you had my husband called over the phone and I know also that Professor Dalle Noci said that it wasn't a good idea at all. Rodolfo went away by his own choice, and you with your new—what do you call them, structures?—shouldn't feel in the least responsible for him." Turning to Fornasier: "And sending up that film director, Ferro—I wonder whether *that* was a very brilliant idea. And listen, Angelantonio, is it true that you have this son, this boy, whom you let grow freely in the wild, up there in Venetia? I don't disapprove at all, mind you, only the idea intrigues me." To Matilde: "And then you told me that the boy was—what word did you use? Demented?"

"*Perhaps* subnormal. Always, always flunked out of school. Only a few days ago, Angelantonio, it was you who suggested the idea of placing him in an institution, considering also that the boy has no mother. There are excellent institutions for recoverable subnormals, in quiet, cheerful locations."

"But I was making fun of you, Matilde," Fornasier said. "You are crazy, and that's one reason why I'm so violently attracted to you. You always want to put everybody in the hospital. A few nights ago I had a dream in which you and I were in the hospital together, in a king-size bed."

"As usual, you are sneering at things which are very serious and profound. So I shall only repeat to you that I care deeply for both you and your son."

Crocetti Vidal, perfectly insulated, is again leafing through the page proofs of the Organigram.

Laura lies in waiting, following his motions, like a favorably placed huntress; then she shoots again: "I heard that you people in charge of this new Group are preparing other periodicals and that there will be one for women called *Mary Jane.* Did you pick that title on purpose? I mean, Mary Jane in Spanish would be Marijuana, and people say the reason you called it that was to, well, camouflage the subject of drugs; I find that very curious and amusing. Another magazine will be aimed at attracting frigid tourists to the Ionian Sea. Right? So I've heard. We have no definite traveling plans, so, frigid or not, out of curiosity we could go to this tourist center you're building on the Ionian Sea."

An insert from Fornasier: "I was there last week and they're still far behind, but if you want . . .

Crocetti Vidal raises his head and distributes smiles and green glances all around, creating total silence. He pounds his fist on the desk, but softly—the delicate gavel striking by a courteous moderator. His eyes stop on Matilde: "Let's recapitulate. You have two basic options: Switzerland and the Ionian coast. The two can easily be integrated into a single project. In Switzerland, with the support of your friend Daphne, you can develop your search, first, for a specialized school for retarded children which our friend Angelantonio, following your report, will take into consideration for his son, Vittorino; and second, for a suitable clinic for Spada, to be selected following the directives which Eugenio Dalle Noci, in the final analysis, will have to coordinate and integrate for you. But your first option, in the immediately chronological sense, is the Ionian coast. There, Elio himself will structure and organize your further movements. Elio Vidal. Even you, Matilde, have never met him; he is very much involved with problems that particularly interest you, namely, the conception of a clinical-touristic complex, and neo-feminist movements. He is my cousin. He has no aptitudes for leadership, he is not executive material. He is a man of ideas. Four doctorates. He is at his best in conducting basic work on projected operations on the most characteristic and most sensitive nuclei of our avant-garde culture. He has been interested in sexology but—as I was saying the other day to Benn and other international representatives of the Group—for the time being Elio is conducting a purely conjectural discourse, which will later be subjected to more extensive reappraisals."

"Does this cousin of yours, Elio, resemble you? Physically, I mean."

Without looking at Laura, Crocetti Vidal rises from his seat like the chairman at the close of a meeting. "Thank you for coming." He walks around his desk to Matilde and embraces her, kissing her on both cheeks. Then he is confronted by Laura, her limpid, gelid eyes raised toward him, her smile intact.

He bends over slightly, but Laura, with her strong hands used to the horse's bridle, grabs his shoulders and holds him at the right distance, scrutinizing him. Then she lifts her face toward him, offering her half-parted lips. Their mouths have barely touched when she lets go of him abruptly and turns her back.

This spring journey is one of the events they most cherish in their lives. They never have a program. This year it was the same as ever.

They left when it was already dark, taking a southeasterly direction. Matilde observed, "After all, we are under Peppino's remote control."

"Of course not. I'm driving."

They stopped at an inn on a high hill; they didn't read the name of the place; in fact they didn't even know what province or region it was. The inn was painted inside and out, with the same white and rough plaster; all of the lighting was fluorescent. It was already three in the morning; intense silence dominated the woody hills all around.

They got a room with a matrimonial bed; they undressed completely and slipped under the sheet and blanket, holding hands.

"I bet you I'll dream about that man Peppino."

Matilde was silent a long while, her eyes open in the dark. Then she decided to confide the secret, in a whisper: "Do you know that he has been chaste all his life?" But by then Laura was sleeping like a log.

She woke up at four in the afternoon and after ten minutes she was in the car, ready to go. She drove with perfect rhythm, a true pupil of her husband, always finding the right direction with the instinct of a hunting dog, finally coming out into that stretch of the Ionian coast where the Group's hotel complexes rose high and motionless. It was dark already, and the buildings under construction didn't look different from ruins. The moon behind rapid clouds cast flashes of light and agitated shadows on the sea.

XIV

"Adele, there are moments when I begin to fear that we have started the search on the wrong foot."

"Don't be unfair to yourself, Camillo."

"No word from the *prefetto* of the province. Girl's mother wandering God knows where, which amounts to saying that she is, by definition, lost. On the other hand, what could we have done? Entrust ourselves to minor officials? Imprudent; inadvisable. Going immediately to the police or to the local *carabinieri*? From bad to worse. Main point: all news must be silenced from high up. Otherwise I can already see it, much to my horror, start along the path of press organs and other even less desirable forms of telecommunication. No, we haven't done the wrong thing. All we need is equilibrium and patience. And who is this man Molisani? We don't even know his first name."

Adele raises her eyes from her knitting. "You've asked yourself that question a hundred times, and I know as much as you do, Camillo."

"I'll go up again to Flora and Bice."

The two old ladies, originally from Lombardy, once employed as domestic help but now living here as nonpaying guests, spend their days reading back issues of magazines and the *Italian Encyclopedia*; they subscribe to art histories published in instalments; on TV they watch everything.

Their little domain, two bedrooms and a living room, is the most comfortable in the house. Camillo Piglioli-Spada looks through the door of the living room. On the shelves, besides the *Encyclopedia* and dozens of knickknacks, the women keep a collection of butterflies under glass. Conspicuous in the room are the TV set and an enormous yellowish photograph of Laura's father wearing the uniform of an artillery officer in 1915.

Camillo Piglioli-Spada settles himself in a small armchair covered with bright flowery material while the two women stand next to him: "A glass of wine, Signor Camillo?"

"All things considered, I'd rather have a drop of tea, thank you. But let this be clear at the start: leaves, not bags."

"For heaven's sake, Signor Camillo, who's ever heard of tea bags?"

The tea is steaming and very aromatic; he drinks it quickly with delight. He clears his throat: "When you heard the sound of that motor, which of the two of you first went to the window?"

"Together."

"Don't you sleep at night? Or was it that motor that woke you up? Are you sure you didn't dream the whole scene? You haven't even been able to say exactly what time it was. I am here to try and make order among the most plausible hypotheses."

"There's only one hypothesis," cries Flora, who is the dryer and more cutting of the two.

Bice is more verbose: "I go to my window and I realize that Flora has gone to hers in exactly the same instant, so I tell her: 'Flora, tell me the truth, didn't you have the same thought that I had?' "

"Which thought? Let's be precise."

"Well, that the Molisani boy had come to take our girl away."

"But you saw only a shadow?"

"Molisani always wears those kind of clothes. Overalls with a fur collar. We thought that perhaps he was going to take the girl out to dance, but considering the fact that they didn't come back, then it's kind of different."

It's twilight and Flora opens the TV. There is an English lesson and the two women start following it with interest, notebooks and pencils on their laps. Then, remembering their guest, whose attention has been captured by the English lesson, they ask whether they can offer him something else. "A drop of wine now, Signor Camillo?"

"A half drop." He sips the wine and goes into a slumber.

Awakening as if from a dream of falls and precipices, he rises abruptly and goes down to his wife. He finds her still seated at the same place, knitting, but standing behind her is a young man, two of his fingertips touching the back of the armchair, looking, it seemed to the ambassador, like Edward, Prince of Wales, beside his mother. Except that this young man is wearing padded overalls and has a round face baked by the sun; all around it, hair and beard form a furry frame, curly and soft.

Stopping on the threshold, the ambassador inquires, "Who is that sheep?"

"Camillo! It's Molisani!"

"And who is he?"

"The boy you were looking for! He came here to pay Genzianella a visit."

"But if Genzianella isn't here? At any rate, he has put his paw into the trap, so to speak. Molisani, are you one of those who belong to that youth revolt movement?"

Molisani shrugs.

"If you don't, why are you dressed like that?" The two glare at each other for a long while. "My niece has disappeared. This piece of information doesn't exactly seem to surprise you. *Et pour cause.*"

"Well, she may have left again; as a matter of fact I wasn't sure I'd find her."

"There, you see? You admit, by implication, that you know something about it. Where was she going? Where is she?"

"Who?"

"My niece."

"Well, what am I supposed to know?"

"Who else should know but you?"

"Well, no, I am the one who doesn't know. If I came here without knowing, that's because I don't know."

"See how you get all mixed up? And don't start every answer with 'Well . . .' like people interviewed on TV. What year are you?"

"Year of what?"

"Aren't you a student? No, you are not. That is to say, I interpret your shrug, and I put it on record, as a negative answer. What's you occupation?"

"Well, I've done different things. Bartending. But I want to be a photographer."

"You've done this, you want to be that. But what are you *now?*" Turning to his wife, affably: "You have to interpret them as though they were animals. Deaf-and-dumb animals, at that."

"Signor Rodolfo is not here?"

"My brother is in isolation in northern Italy. Do you know each other?"

"Well, a little. It was your niece who told me to come here. She always tells me to come when she wants me to come."

"There you go again with your convolutions of evasive words. Do me a favor and try to understand that if I ever take you to the police station, you'll have to provide more precise answers."

"Why?"

"Because in places like that they are not satisfied with vague answers."

"No, what I mean is, why do you want us to go to the police?"

"It's one of the logical places to report the disappearance of a person. In the specific case, a person who has been abducted by another individual; and all evidence points straight to you. Abduction of a minor—keep that in mind. Are you on drugs?"

"No." Again the two exchange long steady looks. Molisani resumes: "Listen, why don't you let *me* look for her? If you go to the police, there may be a messy scandal in the newspapers."

"Hm. You are afraid of that, aren't you?"

"It seems to me he has exactly the same idea as you, Camillo. You can't dismiss these new young men just because they wear beards like that."

The phone rings in the hall.

"The *prefetto,* I bet you anything."

Piglioli-Spada walks out quickly to take the call; he soon comes back slowly. "It was for Bice and Flora: friend of theirs."

Adele whispers cautiously, "I still think we should have tried to reach Laura first of all. She may be a vagabond but she has common sense, and besides, she might give us some other clue."

"The testimony we have so far points to this young man. We could have a police line-up, the American way, but where would we find a sufficient quantity of *barbudos*?"

Then Molisani starts complaining loudly: "Why do you want to do this to me? Leave me in peace. I'm a peaceful man."

Adele, uncertain: "He looks like a mild, innocent young man."

"I am mild and innocent. The thought of the police frightens me. Why do you want to do this? What right do you have to frighten me? Give me something to eat. I'm hungry. When I'm scared I always get hungry."

The ambassador looks at him aghast. He has always conceived of bartenders as men maintaining shady little contacts, without scruples, open to anything. He decides to take Molisani up to Bice and Flora and have him fed, meanwhile studying the reactions of the two ladies face-to-face with the suspect.

The two ladies receive the boy cheerfully and prepare a three-egg omelette for him. They stand next to him to watch him eat. He looks back at them with the expression of a stray animal being given food and shelter. Every time he raises his glass of red wine he toasts the two ladies quickly and shyly.

Piglioli-Spada follows the meal with a fixed but empty gaze. After finishing his second glass of wine, Molisani smiles reassuringly at him and speaks slowly, as if he has concluded a fatiguing series of thoughts: "Look, it would be easier to imagine Spada abducting me."

"Spada. I gather that's what you call my niece."

"Well, yes, among us, in our circle."

"So there is a circle." Turning to the two women: "Well, now, do you recognize him?"

Bice, with pride: "The girl has so many friends. We thought it was he, but . . ."

"But what?"

"But, but," Flora shouts, as if to a deaf man.

The ambassador nods to Molisani, who rises from the table. They go back downstairs together. Adele has interrupted her knitting; she is reading the newspaper of two days ago. Her husband announces, "No results, Adele, but I think it will be wise to keep Molisani here with us, anyway. We'll put him upstairs, in the room where poor Rodolfo used to retire and write his nonsense at the typewriter. You, Molisani, considering that you are a peaceful man, will settle peacefully upstairs. You have all the time you need, and using that typewriter—or, in case my brother has taken it away with him, a pen which I can provide for you—you will compile a list of individuals belonging to the circle, as you call it, of my niece. I presume they will be people more or less corresponding to your physical appearance and following your same habits in regard to dress. You know how to write, don't you?"

"Well, what does this mean? That I must stay on here?"

"I should like to ask you, with a certain amount of firmness, to do me this favor. The only alternative is the police station."

"Then can I find a shelter for my car?"

"That's your problem."

After Molisani has gone out, the ambassador listens intently, fearing the young man might start the car and escape in the night. He hears no sound; soon the young man is back, whistling. He announces, "I've pushed the car into the chapel."

With a long sigh, Piglioli-Spada gets up. "Come, Molisani, I'll show you upstairs."

When he comes down again he sits in front of his wife, and the two keep silent for about twenty minutes. Every now and then the ambassador sighs. Finally he says, "The little chapel is now used as a shelter for automobiles. Genzianella has disappeared. Yet I can't convince myself that all of this is true. *Au fond,* during my whole life, nothing has seemed quite real to me."

"Don't let those foolish thoughts bother you again."

"Now that she has disappeared, I realize that after all, as far as I am concerned, Genzianella never was present. Moreover, I feel that all my friends are like me in their relationships to their fellow human beings. It's as though we had never seen one another. I am wondering why. And now that young man has fallen asleep."

In fact, the sound of powerful snoring descends from upstairs.

"They are like animals, Adele; I warned you."

"At that age. He could be our son, sleeping up there. Same age as our Amedeo." Her husband raises an eyebrow and she corrects herself: "The age Amedeo was when he died."

"Right. Not our son, then. Rather, a grandson, imagining that poor Amedeo had lived and had had a male child."

XV

Rodolfo Spada:

Again my daughter found a letter addressed to me on the kitchen table. In fact, it's what is known as a packet; the sender is young Diego Boldrin. But I am an alien to the world of packets! So my daughter kept it, saying that she will try to read it, maybe aloud with the others, and then perhaps give me a brief synthesis of the amusing passages, provided there are any.

As a matter of fact, it has become our habit here to rule our actions on the basis of the amusement principle. Thus with perfect naturalness and without bothering anyone, we solve problems which are fundamental in the life of a community. I haven't the slightest doubt. A united, cheerful community, its mutual feelings in clear focus. No use attempting further definitions. It's too obvious.

Obvious? Not to Remigio Ferro, apparently. He crouches near me, he scrutinizes me, he questions me with his eyes. Then, suddenly, a cascade of words, a long series of deviations in tangential directions, a breathless flight over lands peopled by irrelevant, but to him obsessive ghosts. One of the scabs he keeps picking at is the failure of the "avant-garde" to recognize his cultural and artistic personality.

He starts abruptly: "It enrages me to see some puny, half-bald, chinless individuals recognized as avant-garde. They grow their hair shoulder-length, and a flourishing beard, and they're all set."

He can't help addressing these wholly meaningless effusions to me.

He starts again: "Trendolini. He is one of the leaders of avant-garde literary operations. Rosario Trendolini. My fellow student at the University of Padua. Now he doesn't even say hello to me, so negligible am I to him. I meet him on the street and I realize he has a *Divine Comedy* under his arm. 'It interests me for some problems of my own,' he says evasively. Among words which I don't understand, he mentions a name I know very well: Arnaut Daniel. I catch Arnaut on the bounce and I start reciting: *'Ieu sui Arnaut, que plor e vau cantan: consiros vei la passada folor . . .'* After I'm through with the whole quotation, I tell him, 'Wonderful lines. As you see, I know them by heart.' Trendolini looks at me with suspicion, cutting me off; he leaves without a word."

"Try to recite those lines to the Spadone twins or to Luigi and they'll follow you with enchantment."

"But don't you see my problems?"

"No." I try to comfort him: "Now you'll go to jail and they'll make all the noise you want about you."

"If they put me in jail, the Trendolinis of this world will find me more insignificant than ever; they don't appreciate a man who is ready to face the consequences of his personal conduct, even to the point of ending up behind bars. I haven't got a lira, but they, on the other hand, live extraordinarily well. Nowadays there's a de-luxe avant-garde. At the origin of extremely advanced cultural-political operations there's always a substantial core of capital, and if there wasn't that —good-bye, revolutionaries of the written and the spoken word!"

"I don't see why you waste time worrying about mundane affairs."

He doesn't listen to me. "For that matter, could you imagine a revolution here even in the good old sense of the word? No. And do you know why? Because it would go unnoticed. Suppose they would dislodge the industrial magnate from his villa with its private park and Olympic-size pool, and carry him to the public square, spit on him, chop his head off between the Marco and Todaro columns as in the days of the Venetian Republic, or shoot him at the spot on the docks in Naples where they executed the revolutionaries of 1799. Well, people wouldn't notice; they would troop on toward the motorboat for the Lido or the hydrofoil to Capri."

Apparently he doesn't consider me attentive enough, so he tries a higher pitch: "Think of your friend Daphne, dripping with culture, at the very center of charity organizations to promote the arts, always in the forefront—yesterday it was Alienation, today it's Ecology—all made possible by the fortune of one of her now-deceased husbands. And he himself didn't understand anything but Puccini. He had a stereo system installed in his Rolls Royce and listened to one Puccini opera after another, wandering at night through the vast plains of Texas."

"I've met him. First-rate man. Excruciating detail: he died of cancer of the throat just like Puccini."

Ferro looks at me with distrust and attempts an even higher pitch: "You try to stick to human values in situations, but don't kid yourself. The only success that counts is financial success, banks, investments, and needless to say, real estate."

Evidently this piece of information doesn't sufficiently excite me. Then he really starts yelling, in the tone of a challenge: "Consider Crocetti Vidal; he is the key man in a very opulent Group and his ideal is obvious: organizing and implementing avant-garde cultural operations. Today, that's the road to power. Boldrin is kidding himself. I'm referring to your pupil, Diego Boldrin."

"Yes, yes," I say quickly, and I realize in a flash, but with a half-hour delay—very unusual for me—that I should immediately have thrown away the Boldrin packet rather than let the boys and girls open it.

Ferro, in closing: "Culture is damnation. After all, I envy those who manage to be satisfied, to get complete psychological fulfillment, from a purely economic-financial success."

Our conversations, so rambling and redundant, amuse us in the end; we become friends; I enjoy friendship madly.

I comfort him: "You'll land on your feet. Don't give up. Keep your eye on the ball. As of today, there's such a lack of brain power that if you care to put yourself on the intellectual market you can with very little effort become one of the five or six men recognized as the most intelligent of the era."

Then he abandons himself to the most unbridled extravagance: "How right I was in coming here. I need your esteem. To me it's life, it's oxygen. I understand Diego Boldrin's devotion to you. Boldrin's idea of paradise would be making love to Laura, to Genzianella, to Daphne, not so much because they're beautiful women as because they are, respectively, your wife, your daughter and your former mistress, so he would identify with you through those women who are like magic beings to him."

I interrupted this curious talk as I answered a distinct telepathic call from upstairs. It should be noted that no voice or sound came from there. But I rushed up.

I immediately saw the Boldrin packet open on the table, like the jar of barbiturates half emptied in the suicide's room. They had read a good deal of it already. Full of reports on

Group business, of documents, of Xerox memos from B.G.C.V.'s office. In short: an open source of contagion.

And, in fact, there was Vittorino stretched out on a sofa, with my daughter kneeling at his side. One of the Spadone twins and Luigi were standing nearby. The other twin came in bringing ice. I held my hand on Vittorino's forehead to estimate his temperature at one hundred and three, which the thermometer confirmed. My daughter started massaging his forehead with ice, then following with soft, cool kisses.

XVI

The immense main building of the Ionian tourist center is still uninhabitable, but there are rooms already furnished in smaller buildings. Laura and Matilde wake up in one of these and press various bell buttons, but the silence is total, nobody turns up. They go down without washing, in search of something to eat.

Out in the open they find themselves standing on a wide flat cement square, violently hit by the sun, with a very intense sea in the background.

A young man, not tall but solid, in full city dress and with the unsure gait of the displaced person, is walking on the incandescent cement toward them. Seen at close range, he turns out to be blond and with a tremendous head, sad blue eyes behind enormous glasses, a smile more sorrowful than ironical on his full lips. They ask him where they can find food.

"Good day, dear ladies." The young man's speech is nasal and precise, yet timid. "Your arrival had been announced via teletype by the executive secretary-general, Dr. Crocetti Vidal, and I in my humble way was fervently expecting you. On the problem of victuals I cannot yet answer you. I arrived recently myself, with orders, good heavens, to instruct myself on the preliminary studies conducted here by Elio Vidal on what the Group describes as behavioral patterns of the Mediterranean tourist. As is often the case, the Group's computers were fed with very inexact data concerning my person: for example, it was communicated to those innocent machines that I have studied sociology, whereas I am, in the final analysis, a philologist."

"You are very young, though." Laura hasn't understood a word of the stranger's talk and she is only trying to say something that would put him at ease. Since he hasn't introduced himself, she encourages him: "What did you say your name was?"

"My name, dear lady, will mean absolutely nothing to you. I am Diego Boldrin. The firm, merged now into the Group, treats me like a schoolboy or even a little serf, but *non praevalebunt.*"

"As a matter of fact, I believe I've heard your name mentioned. By Crocetti Vidal, you know?"

"I would feel honored only if you had told me that you had heard it mentioned by Rodolfo Spada, your husband and my only true teacher."

Laura to Matilde: "He's a darling. I have the impression that this young man Boldrin is really a darling person." To the young man: "Thank you, stay with us, help us a little. And this Elio Vidal, Peppino's cousin, where is he?"

"He is flying back to the nest this very moment." Boldrin performs a magician's gesture, half triumphant, half diabolical, toward the sky, pointing to a helicopter in rapid descent.

In a matter of seconds the helicopter, agile and glowing, lands on the vast cement square. First the pilot disembarks, then a very large man wearing a T-shirt and jeans. The closer he comes, the better they can see that he is tanned, hairy, and looking very much like Crocetti Vidal, but blown up, his physical traits almost monstrously accentuated, including the rich skin lubrication.

"Forgive me." He kisses the ladies' hands. "I am Elio Vidal. Peppino told me everything." Laura observes a soft lightness in his manner, in his touch. She is attracted by those qualities, not unusual in a fat man. She asks where they can get something to eat.

"Complete American breakfast. I'll prepare it myself."

He leads the way back into the building where the women have been sleeping. Inside, through a series of white, glittering, rather hospital-like corridors whose existence they had not suspected, he leads them to a kitchen done in imitation farm style but fully electrified. Vidal's thick fingers, Laura notices, move with the same soft dexterity as his whole body: in a matter of minutes he has scrambled a dozen eggs, fried many thick slices of bacon, and toasted wheat bread. He serves the food himself, with a dancer's mimicry. And he acts as cupbearer, pouring orange juice into tall glasses.

They all eat avidly except Boldrin, who often interrupts his already slow mastication, wipes his mouth and bombards Vidal with well-articulated, nasal, slow and inexorable words: "My dear Dr. Vidal, I'll start by saying, superfluously I'm sure, that you see in me an insignificant specimen of a collaborator outside the Organigram. Curiously enough, the Group has financed my trip here so I could gather information and instruct myself, and a sense of duty compels me to ask you some questions. What can you tell me about the behavioral patterns of the Ionian tourist? And, before I forget, about the motivational basis for a clinical-touristic structure such as this?" Vidal smiles, his mouth full. Boldrin turns to the two women: "The Group, my dear ladies, is secretly planning this structure on the splendid Ionian coast not only as a simple clinical-touristic *complex* but also"—he laughs aridly and lugubriously—"as a place for the *treatment* of certain *complexes.*"

Matilde, amiably but as an examiner preparing a secret trap: "What are you alluding to exactly, Boldrin?"

"To the complexes of sexual incompetence. To therapeutic activities for bringing about erotic release in unhappy couples. Am I right? In the most advanced countries, like the United States and, presumably, Japan and West Germany, there are clinics for couples who haven't been able to reach an adequate erotic pitch and who are advised, instructed, guided to that goal. Apparently they're having a smashing success. I've heard that they keep a certain number of experts, of able male and female initiators who experiment until the couple is in a position to find the right way unaided. Isn't that so, Vidal?"

But Elio's mouth is full again. Matilde replies "Boldrin, you are too intelligent to lower yourself to the level of those puerile individuals who have been speaking of 'sex clinics' and perhaps even of 'little therapeutic orgies,' and for that matter, Crocetti Vidal I'm sure didn't fail to make it clear to you that the Group has so far dealt with such projects only at a hypothetical level. On the other hand, you know better than I do that wherever such projects have actually been put into practice, they have already shown extremely convincing results."

"You don't have to convince me, I'm with you already, Professor Apicetta. Whereas, frankly, Dr. Vidal, your plans for a music-festival, a symposium on structuralist criticism, and such, leave me totally indifferent, as they do everyone else, of course. I would not include them among the motivational structures . . ."

Laura interrupts: "That's quite right, I find. By now every village, however remote, has its own art prize or festival.

That's the very reason why I wish you would go on, Boldrin, on the subject of erotic release, or whatever you called it, which is something much more—I don't know—alive . . . I find. Right? You, for instance, Vidal, would you be one of those sex experts?"

Vidal, slowly, with a warm voice: "You must realize, signora, that I don't know how to speak well. I study. Every once in a while I write an article for the reviews which deal with my themes, liberation, liberating techniques. I'll give you reprints and I'll put the statistical material at your disposal."

Without grasping the meaning of his words, Laura affectionately squeezes his arm: "What an extraordinary man you are, Elio."

Then Elio takes the two women and Boldrin to visit another building, smaller and completely furnished. Here they walk on wall-to-wall carpets. Modern etchings hang on the wood-paneled walls. And there are lamps with brass stands, and potted palms, rigid in the conditioned air. Through the thick window glass they see faintly green olive trees moved by the wind, and stretches of blue sea.

Vidal explains: "This villa will be surrounded by bungalows, and the whole will constitute the area that has a more definitely therapeutic coloring. Heated swimming pools too, very relaxing." At that point he reveals a slight stammer, an emotional disturbance which only comes, as he explains, in sporadic attacks.

The shiny white doors to the rooms have rich brass doorknobs. Vidal turns one of them to reveal a room bathed in dark-blue light, a kind of astral penumbra. In the large bed, very new but antique in style, an old man is sleeping, with a serene smile on his roseate, florid face.

"Let's not wake him up." Vidal shuts the door. "How well

he sleeps. How good he looks. So healthy. He's my pa-pà. Our diets work so beautifully. He's almost ninety. I'm quite the opposite of Peppino. Peppino was born when his pa-pà was nineteen, I when mine was past sixty. You saw, didn't you, how beautiful he is?"

Matilde asks, "What do you give him?"

"Pap mainly, but not only the royal pap, which is the nourishment of the queen bee, but various others too, studied by the Group, which has a polyglot magazine of gerontology and dietetics."

Matilde in a sing-song: "I confess I hadn't expected such an interesting place. Do you suppose it might be a good idea, Lauretta, to take it into consideration for poor Rodolfo? It might be even better than a simple neurological hospital."

They are walking along the corridor with regular steps made silent by the carpet; Boldrin now stops so abruptly that they all do the same.

"Dr. Vidal, this is it: now we have truly reached the limit."

They keep silent, waiting for Boldrin to explain, but as he doesn't seem to be adding anything, Matilde asks, "What limit?"

The young man looks around, satisfying himself that he has obtained a nice background of silence against which his talk can stand out conspicuously: "Professor Apicetta, Dr. Vidal, Signora Spada, last week in Rome I was received, in his office in the new glass-and-steel building of the firm, by the secretary-general and secular arm of the Group, Benito Giuseppe Crocetti Vidal. My memory retains words with photographic precision; I have learned the technique from Rodolfo Spada, my only true teacher. 'Dear Boldrin,' the secretary-general told me, 'I suppose that you, like all of us, are aware of a new need for clarification of the issues, for incisive contributions to productive dialogue. Positions of ambiguity are not tolerable. Concerning our structure at the level of personnel employment I must provide the Group with realistic options, concrete guidelines for decisively selective action.' It was his way of telling me that I wasn't going to get into the Organigram. I knew that already, and for that matter, in the Organigram I would feel myself in a straitjacket.''

Elio winks at the ladies: "Boldrin is the leader of dissent."

"The language of the executive secretary-general is much less banal, Dr. Vidal. He has said, and the message has been publicized through thousands of Xerox copies: 'We must always avoid any sharp polarization of the issues. Our method is only one: the free and varied articulation of our basic thought patterns.' Finally I managed to inform him of the main reason for my visit: 'You are losing your best men. I didn't come to speak of myself but of a master, Rodolfo Spada. A man in close touch with the nature of things.' And the executive secretary-general, clearly without listening: 'Your definitions of Spada are excellent. Write us a report; it will be included in the Spada file, which is maintained in a semiactive though nonorganic position. Our good Spada is outside our restructuring process, but his reactivation in a different key is not wholly inconceivable.'

"I fled, as he himself fled on a distant day. Before going, I made a tour of the offices. No one I could talk to about Spada. And then I also realized that a word of admiration and affection from me would be the kiss of death.

"Not to mention our personal files; they are actual, thick police dossiers on all, I repeat, all of the Group's employees present and past, whether or not they be structuralized and organigraphed. There is internal espionage on a large scale, masterminded by Dr. Peritti and by his young aide whose name, aptly enough, means 'little eye,' Dr. Occhietto. At the summit, everything comes to a head in secret investigation services on both sides of the Atlantic. All international police forces are following the media day and night. Every piece of writing produced by us, from our first journalistic steps to the present, is placed on file, word by word, processed by computer, classified; every phone call we make is taped by the wire-tapping services and all will be used against us.

"One example? It has been announced that the Vice-President of a superpower nation—I won't say which, because even walls have ears—is going to visit Europe; and the secret services maintain that they have evidence of a plan to kidnap that personage, a plan which should apparently go into operation during his visit to Venice. Even the papers have carried stories about the existence of an organization specializing in the kidnaping of Vice-Presidents. Now, I am sure that, following indications given by the Group's investigators, Dr. Peritti and Dr. Occhietto, every piece of writing, every allusion, every small hint we may have made about this Vice-President will be transmitted to the computers and projected into the context of our whole work and of all of our ideas and opinions with which the computers have been, as they say, fed. It has occurred to me, for example, that an article by Rodolfo Spada on what he called "televisionary political campaigns" contained an incidental remark on the Vice-President in question, where he was described as a polyglot with a profound historical-philosophical education, a thinker, whose sharp, experienced eye pierces the international political scene, a refined orator in the great Greek tradition of Lysias and Demosthenes . . .

"Electronic computers, signora, possess minds which are more acute than those of the Group officials who interrogate them. So there will be the vibration of the alarm bell, the flashing of the sulphurous light, the blitz-reading of those words and their immediate classification in the category of diabolically satirical and crypto-subversive attacks. Predictably, fatally, there will be accusations of conspiracy in the vice-presidential kidnaping plans. Oh, they'll accuse us of anything. They'll grab any chance to put us in the net which is being woven to ensnare us. The forces of repression are organizing in secret leagues. The masters' plot. The powerful, which in historical tradition were the victims of conspiracies, now become conspirators themselves, to do us in. At the firm, I tried to shake those who I thought were friends; nothing to be done, there is nothing concretely human in their heads. I am alone, Signora Spada. But what are *you* planning to do?"

"In what way, Boldrin?" Of his talk she has understood little or nothing, but Boldrin's fervor excites her.

"I've sent your husband some rather innocuous material; I don't dare commit the worst to the mails. I'll go up to Venetia and I'll implore him to listen to me. They tell me he's isolated and doesn't keep in touch with the world. I'm looking for people who may help me in persuading Spada to accept the leadership. But now, hearing you all talk, I am nonplused. I didn't believe it could come to this. If I understand you well, you want to have him liquidated, shut up as if he were mentally ill."

"We had thought of one of those relaxation homes; you know? Dalle Noci, who has examined him, thought of something in Switzerland."

"Spada, mentally ill? He, the very splendor of reason?"

"You are very dear, Boldrin."

"Signora, then tell me only one thing: Where is your daughter? I met her a few times in Rome—an astonishing apparition. I feel that I'd be able to communicate with her." Boldrin has a lump in his throat. "Forgive me, but here I've lost all hopes. The main reason I came here, signora, is that I knew I would have a chance to talk to you. But I've lost . . . Forgive . . ." His lips tremble.

"I absolutely agree with you that Genzianella is rather marvelous and I'm sure the two of you would get along beautifully. You, Boldrin, are a very picturesque young man with great resources, and my daughter is at Succaso with her uncle and aunt, who are not exactly the most amusing people the world has to offer."

"Dr. Vidal, forgive me, but I can't breathe in here. Do you suppose I could borrow a pair of swimming trunks? Do you mind if I take a dip in the sea before leaving?"

"Now that I was going to show you the pool?" Vidal opens a sliding door and reveals an immense gymnasium, at its center a marble swimming pool with statues at both ends—abstract forms, but reminiscent of human nudes. From the vast water surface, white thermal steam arises. In the water, men and women wearing large light robes as in a river baptism are swimming slowly with synchronized motions as in a ballet lesson. They murmur rather than sing inaudible words in unison.

Matilde, as if recognizing a work of art which she had only known through photographs: "Oh, oh, how interesting."

Boldrin's voice is suffocated but frenetic: "Dr. Vidal, what about my swimming trunks?"

Nobody listens to him. Vidal, enormous and more than ever shining with perspiration in the steamy air, smiles with pride: "Come upstairs and see, I've got very attractive little things."

They go up a staircase made of iron, as on ships. The upper floor is divided into several rooms. Or rather than like rooms, they look like stalls at a trade fair. The walls seem to be movable partitions.

"Everything here is temporary and experimental; I've just started." Vidal guides his guests toward the last of those sections, the largest, with only a rapid wave of the hand as they pass by the smaller sections. They hear him murmur formulas like "recreational therapy" or "kinetic artifacts." The visitors catch a few glimpses, here of a large glass parallelepiped filled with green water, algae and exotic fish; there of a giant abacus in vivid colors: the small spheres, electrified, are like colored bulbs; and then, in a dark alcove, a framed rectangle of glass, like a large TV screen, where abstract shapes—roseate, lively, carnal—compose and decompose, a continuous variety of sinuous motions against a background of soft monotonous music.

"We'll come back later, but first I want to show you this." Vidal precedes them into the largest section. Here a window offers a limited view of the outside world, trees, the sea.

But inside, the place is occupied by a very wide hilly landscape lined by a complicated railroad network, the whole in perfect miniature. Vidal activates some electric switches, and the little trains, scattered all over that railroad landscape, start moving with the regular and patient exactness of ants, continuously entering into and emerging from tunnels covered with rich vegetation, disappearing into one of those holes and reappearing at the other end.

"Don't you love my tunnels made of meadow grass? Doesn't it make you feel you want to enter deep into them? Or even eat, devour them? The toy-train collection is mine, I put it together over twenty years and I'm donating it to the Group. In fact, they're such extraordinary things that it's a bit grotesque to call them toys. Rather pop art. In the arts now there are splendid new ideas every day and I'll employ them a good deal. Liberating function. I've been liberated all my life, I was born liberated, so I devote myself to these . . ."

Boldrin interrupts him ever more urgently: "Dr. Vidal, trunks or no trunks, I'm going to take my dip. Then I'll go directly to my car, so I'll take leave now, from you and from these kind ladies." To Laura: "I'll be heading toward Succaso. Toward your daughter. I feel she and I will communicate."

"I'm sure of that, Boldrin."

Through the thick window glass they see him shortly afterward run naked among the trees, and far away, jump into the waves.

They seem not to notice him. Matilde to Vidal: "Elio, I should like to get some orientation. Give me your material and your articles to read."

"I'll give you everything, Matilde."

Laura cuts in: "I seem to understand that in order to produce this thing, this erotic release, you'll also employ people who can give help, who can offer themselves and work so as to turn these blocked individuals in the right direction. For example, Elio, would I be good for that?"

"We don't pose problems of that sort as yet; we have not reached the level of specific selections." Vidal looks at her intensely.

"Yes, but if someday . . . Women employed like that . . . I don't know, well, I must say I would envy them a little bit. I don't know whether I would envy them because of their evident know-how . . . or because the idea of being so simply, so naturally available . . . Right?"

Now Vidal looks at both his visitors and there is a long silence, broken only by the sound of his thick, fast breathing. In silence he takes them again to the pool, now empty; a quiet, white vapor rises from it.

"You have no idea how relaxing and harmonizing this is. Now we'll undress, I'll give you the right costumes and I'll teach you a few exercises."

Matilde asks, "Are you really sure, Elio?"

"I am," says Laura.

Vidal's eyes and hers suddenly meet, warm and surprised.

XVII

Rodolfo Spada:

At last all goes perfectly well. My predictions have been fulfilled down to the minute. Vittorino has no fever, he has regained his color, his speech, everything. While he was delirious we couldn't understand a word he said. It was excruciating, but we didn't allow ourselves to be weakened by pity, however intense. Absolute efficiency on the part of his friends and myself. I felt as if through Vittorino's pain I were reexperiencing all the pains I have ever felt in my life. And the nights when he was delirious in the dark among nightmares were all the nights of childish fear in this world concentrated into one. Seeing him lost in suffering, I had to press my heart to prevent it from breaking or collapsing.

But I know the right pills and potions too. Which, of course, are not enough; the boy needed also to feel strong doses of human reality around him; this was provided by everybody through simple natural impulse. The Spadone twins are born nurses, with an absolute and instinctive capacity for effective and silent contact with the suffering person. All of them are more experienced than Vittorino.

One of the twins sometimes goes and stays awhile in Venice, where she is in touch with students, including foreign ones. Luigi has wandered a lot, to Padua and elsewhere, also in the Friuli and Istria regions. I think he was expelled from the local school, rather than simply flunking out.

More than once already, listening to governmental or executive-level talk on TV, Vittorino and the others had been overwhelmed by an irrepressible mixture of laughter and weeping which unsettled them for some time and made them look feverish. The others would recover soon, finding again their human speech and a sense of reality; Vittorino had a more difficult time.

Now Vittorino has paid for everybody. His case was like that of the noble savage, who needed only one simple germ of the common cold brought by the civilizers into the paradisal South Seas to develop immediate lethal fevers. Before spraying the Boldrin packet with alcohol and throwing it into the flames, I let my eye fall on the material in Xerox, and I caught phrases here and there: *selective decisional choices . . . polarization . . . essentializing basic themes . . . conditioned reactivation . . .* For Vittorino, who has always lived here and has not been adequately immunized by TV and newspapers, the sudden contact with ample doses of those unrealities was too violent. Hence his terrible illness. I haven't the slightest doubt.

Before losing himself in undecipherable delirium, he would insistently repeat to us certain phrases of his own, interspersed with deep sighs: "I am in a state of total stupidity." Or: "There it goes, way over there, the joy and the sweetness of our life." Or, with resignation: "Uh, Father. Uh, chocolate cake." As if he mentioned goods forever lost. Genzianella, after spoon-feeding him lemon sherbet made by her, kissed him on the mouth and he said, "In this moment I do not remember the future any more." Then we lost him.

Day and night he was our only concern. Now, as I said, he is very well, all surrounded by general attention, especially feminine, kisses, caresses. My daughter says that Vittorino is a kind of Molisani, only more beautiful besides being more rubicund and incomparably more imaginative. "My child, you're made of gold," she tells him.

When our boy was already getting better, a magnificent old lady, a total stranger, made her appearance; or rather, as I went down to the ground floor I found her already settled, planted in the middle of the room: "I am Countess Spadone. Countess. The whole thing is a big joke. What very sweet children. Everything today is sweeter than it used to be. I am the grandmother of those little girls who love you so. This villa is ours. Angelantonio bought it for a few pennies, but what does that have to do with it? It's the Villa Spadone, our own. Angelantonio, who is very sweet, understands this perfectly."

According to the twins, in all that the lady says there is not a word of truth in regard to property, lineage or aristocratic titles. It seems she was a peasant who later became a stage actress. Her very attractive discourse is a fabric of mythicized information. She is a grandmother by definition, inasmuch as the middle generation has been cut out by wars, international and civil. Her son was Count Spadone, a legendary figure around these fields, these lagoons. "The young men from the Venetia of those years, they're all dead."

I would bet anything that Remigio Ferro will maintain that this old lady has been invented by him. We'll let him say so. If anything, she has invented herself. Besides, she has a wide spiderweb of family relationships in which her memory gets caught, then bounces here and there from thread to thread: "My Passina cousins. They lost Diomede, not in the war though, and of course it would have been the first one, the Great War; they lost him later, in a motorcycle accident. At that time I still sang quite well, I dedicated an evening of songs to them. 1923. Here at the villa. A kind of wake, of funeral lament; very sweet. So many dead! For instance, the *arditi* corps. You know, the ones with a dagger between their teeth? Reckless. But then also among the poor, you know. We had two valets, brothers, with starched white jackets, very much resembling each other and also resembling my ancestors, illegitimate children of some Spadone, I imagine. One of the two died among daggers, hand grenades, barbed wire; not a crown of thorns but a bed of thorns—such guts! The other one lingered at our house for decades, with the air of the wise old gentleman, getting to look more and more like our religious novelist, Fogazzaro. Oh, his handwriting was so much more beautiful than mine! Sweet. A little bit authoritarian toward me, but with so much sweetness deep inside. Do you play music here? You should play much, much music."

She arranged a celebration, with music and all, for Vittorino's recovery. The boy, by his suffering, has reinforced our solidarity and our cheerfulness.

One of the Spadone twins has learned to play the guitar. She was taught by students in Venice, and she plays with grace and energy. All around me in the evening I see lively eyes reflecting the flames on which food is being cooked. Ferro, in a bamboozled state of well-being, is caressing a Spadone twin. Embracing couples disappear in the night while the lady says, "It's beautiful, it's romantic; oh, do as I used to do, abandon your heart to total ecstasy, to lovely debauchery too . . . oh, God, have I said too much? Rodolfo, what a beautiful name—Rudolph, Rudi—have I said too much? Nowadays I'm content to look and listen. Thank you. Blissful nights."

I was almost going to forget: in the middle of the festivities, Angelantonio Fornasier arrived. He started to weep: "I

should have come earlier, to my sick child. I'm a weakling."
The fact is that as a genius he does have telepathic intuitions, but out of phase. Eating and drinking copiously, he kept repeating, "I'm a weakling. Seeing him suffer would destroy me. He reminds me too much of my wife."

His wife. Vittorino's mother. A Russo-Chilean woman whom he knew and loved in South America, dead shortly after Vittorino's birth. Angelantonio breaks into sobs when he speaks of her, but it's a robust kind of sobbing, a vigorous homage to his memories. I won't even try to reproduce his words; the very act of writing them down would mar them. Nor could I reproduce his tone, which I would describe as one of exultant melancholy.

The Spadone twins look and listen ecstatically as if he were telling a fable full of deep meanings. The Fornasier boy in my daughter's arms stares into empty space with his clear and actually rather Slavic eyes; he says several times in a deep adult voice, "The mother, the mother."

Angelantonio seemed very happy with the work that the boys and girls have been doing in the house, and generally with life here. Being a genius, he has got the picture in a flash and approves happily, effusively kissing Countess Spadone and pinching the twins. He has read with joy several of our "memos."

By the way. One of our "memos" has appeared on a poster at the Caerne school, reproduced in big red block letters, *not by us:*

Kaiser Wilhelm of Germany and Czar Nicholas of Russia, who must be considered among the major fomenters of a war in which for several years their subjects butchered each other by the tens of millions, were relatives; in private they spoke English, calling each other Willy and Nicky.

I assure Angelantonio that we'll keep an eye on Caerne, but that the Brusò school is no good. The humanities teacher is a fool; while the teacher of mathematics doesn't know how to add and subtract, he cannot even invent some imaginative formula; and as for the French teacher, though she can't produce a single correct sentence in French, she always flunks everybody. Finally, the science teacher is the one who once threw Luigi out of the classroom because the boy had brought him the photograph of a very peculiar flea's leg gigantically blown up, and when the teacher asked where he had got it from, Luigi answered, "From Texas." The teacher thought he was being ridiculed. Not at all, *it was true.*

We wandered one whole afternoon through these lands and waters with perfect delight, except when, on our way home, Angelantonio brought up the subject of the Group. He mentioned new chapters in the Crocetti Vidal saga, and when I asked him, in all sincerity, who this person was, he became alarmed and said that he and I must have a serious talk. Some of the decisions made by the Group in the process of Restructuring, he said, don't please him one bit. With ever livelier sincerity I expressed my doubts on the objective *existence* of this Group.

But he marched on: "Take for instance the way they're treating Boldrin; I don't like it at all. A man like Peritti, if you wish, is nothing but a snake; but Boldrin!" Then he moved on to the subject, if I remember correctly, of "Mediterranean tourist projects."

I had to stop him. "Angelantonio, if you want to go on with this kind of talk, you may do so, but you must realize that *I do not perceive your words.* I repeat, do it, but forgive me if I get up and leave. Believe me, it's the same whether I'm here or somewhere else. On the contrary, if you changed the subject, even though being somewhere else I would perceive from the distance your re-entry into reality, and I would come back and listen to you with delight."

He stares at me but doesn't seem to understand my words, though they are as simple and clear as can be. Fortunately, at this point it was getting to be dinnertime and everybody appeared, first of all the twins announcing the menu. I say to Angelantonio, "I've never eaten better in my whole life, and compared to Rome or Paris, we spend nothing."

He threw himself on the polenta and sausage like everyone else, and on the very pleasant wine from his cellar; but he kept watching me with anxiety and suspicion. Right after dinner he had to leave, and I accompanied him to his car. We embraced and he couldn't help whispering, "There are things I'll have to make you understand whether you like it or not. They don't want to give you a single lira in retirement payments. There are a tremendous number of problems."

Seeing that his words did not reach me, he started the motor of his very powerful British car. Before he got away, I said, "See that you don't get killed, will you?" He is a good driver but not a superlative one.

XVIII

"I am beginning to feel a little bit better, Adele."

"I said that to you from the beginning but you wouldn't listen. Genzianella's disappearance has set you in motion, Camillo, and therefore you feel better."

"I said 'a little bit better.' "

"Feeling the presence of this boy Molisani in the house has helped you, and then all of this coming and going of young men." In the evening twilight Adele is glancing at a paper a few days old.

"That is not the reason, Adele. It pains me to say it, but if anything, it's precisely Genzianella's absence that gives me a minimum of relief and well-being. Now that she is no longer among us—how shall I put it—I see the picture more clearly. Very pretty girl, yet I realize that deep underneath she's always given me the impression of a little monster. It isn't her fault; hm, the way she's been raised. Once upon a time they used to be virgins, obedient, or at any rate that was the criterion, it was the norm; now there is no norm and we are neither here nor there. Neither the convent nor the brothel, so to speak. And yet, if you come to the gist of it, I should say that they do not have much fun. Also when it comes to their sex life, I mean. But then, it's impossible to understand, because though their vocabulary is extremely limited and primordial, they do not communicate; they are banal, yet mysterious."

"You are tormenting yourself with thoughts that don't concern you, Camillo."

"I'm not tormenting myself at all, I'm only asking: How do they manage to understand each other? Deaf-and-dumb animals, I have already provided you with that definition. Maria Laura is like them, though she's much farther on in age. And as if all of this were not enough, my dear relatives are falling apart financially. The condominium apartment in Rome is all covered with mortgages, and as for Succaso, I keep it going. It seems that with the nonsense he used to write, my brother earned a few pennies; now he has stopped writing and they have nothing. Maria Laura—and it grieves me to relate this—is rumored to be more or less indirectly kept by lovers, both masculine and feminine. Beautiful finale. If only my father were here. But the best are dead. In a way, the dead have done the smart thing. I'm only half—"

His wife wakes up, she had been dozing over her old newspaper. "You're half what, Camillo?"

"Dead, Adele."

"Not at all. In fact, this coming and going of young men has done you good."

"It's the second time you use that expression. There's no coming and going; I'm questioning a few of them, at the right intervals."

The half-dozen young men conducted here by Molisani, spaced at about two a day, have all shown very good manners. No one has been able to give the slightest bit of information about Genzianella. Every now and then during the questioning, Piglioli-Spada would interrupt them: "You act like ignoramuses but you don't know me, I shall not be fooled. Watch out or we'll go to the police station." They smile, though mildly frightened.

The young man with a black beard and blue eyes who has been brought this evening turns out to be the son of an old colleague in diplomacy, Brunetti. "But of course, now I know who you are," said the ambassador, I remember you as a tiny little baby at our embassy in Bucharest. What has your father been doing since he retired?"

"He's been lying on his back, perfectly stiff."

"Forgive me, I should have remembered that he died last year, but you have a way of expressing yourself which I find quite absurd. Do you hear the sound of a motor? Don't tell me there are other visits scheduled for this evening?"

"None that we know of." Molisani and Adele exchange tender smiles.

"And can you hear these hurried steps? Since Genzianella disappeared, at each new arrival Bice and Flora throw themselves down the stairs to see who it is."

After a moment the mingled voices of the two women are heard from the courtyard, followed by an isolated male voice, nasal, distinct, penetrating: "I haven't the slightest objection, my dear ladies, to giving you my name. But I am most certain that it will mean absolutely nothing to you. I am Diego Boldrin."

Then there is Flora's cry in the darkness: "The journalist!"

When Boldrin is admitted into the house he looks aghast, shut between the two women as between two walls.

Bice offers him to the ambassador like a juicy morsel: "Signor Camillo, this young man is Diego Boldrin, the journalist."

"Hm, think of that."

Irritated by the irony, Flora yells, "He's one of those who know everything—on kidnapings, seizures, hijackings!"

The ambassador scrutinizes Boldrin without much interest. "I see"—good manners force him to make conversation—"I see. If I understand correctly, you are a specialist in the seizure of people and of airplanes. Such enterprises are now quite in vogue and I shall hasten to add that I, who am opposed to the death penalty, essentially for theological reasons, would, however, favor life sentences for the perpetrators of such actions, without possibility of *bail* or *parole,* to use your terminology."

"Whose terminology?"

"In the very small vocabulary which you people possess, seventy or eighty percent is American. Will you deny that?"

"Mr. Ambassador, I don't dare decide exactly what you are talking about."

"Too bad. I knew very well that one cannot communicate even the most elementary ideas to you. But now, Signor Boldrin, do me a favor and at least make an attempt to tell me what you came here for. I hear from Signora Bice that you are a journalist. If by any chance you came here in that capacity, my advice to you is to leave immediately, considering that from us you'll get absolutely nothing. Zero. No comment. If, on the other hand, the reasons for your presence here are the same for which I have detained Molisani and Brunetti, I warn you that you are of little or no use to us: we look for bearded men wearing overalls, whereas you are freshly shaved and *tiré aux quatre épingles.* "

"Forgive me, Your Excellency, but while you talk I continue to understand very little, except for your initial question—why did I come here. I didn't come as a journalist. I came as a devoted friend of your brother, Rodolfo Spada; to talk about him."

"Then I'm afraid you've been knocking at the wrong door. I shelved my brother a number of years ago."

A grandfather clock strikes the hour. Signora Adele unobtrusively gets up. Respectful of the lady's reserve, Molisani and Brunetti rise and bow in silence. Boldrin, already standing, bows too. After the lady is gone, he resumes: "Mr. Ambassador, I'll try to conform to your language. And I'm telling you that if you have shelved your brother, well, now it's time to pull out his file and re-examine it." He produces a quick, hard laugh. "Hm. The dossier." There is a long, incredulous silence, which evidently irritates him. He must find a way to shake up these sleepy marmots. Boldrin points a finger at Bice and Flora: "These ladies' words seem very alarming to me. It is well known that I am a follower of Rodolfo Spada; well, in announcing me to you, these ladies immediately associated my name with stories of seizures and kidnapings. We are within the area of those pernicious follies which characterize our time."

"Signor Boldrin, here perhaps I perceive a glimmer of a chance to establish communication with you. Which particular follies are you referring to, among so many?"

"Rumors have been spreading, on this and the other side of the Atlantic, about plans for the kidnaping of very eminent persons, particularly persons *in a vice-presidential position.* A very extended network is supposed to exist, one of its centers being in the Venetian region. This may surprise Your Excellency, since the Venetian region is usually considered tame and reactionary. Ha, ha! *We are all on file at the police!* Now, leaving my own person aside, I'll eclipse myself in front of the master, of Rodolfo Spada, I won't even mention the fact that *I am a Venetian* besides being practically a pariah in the eyes of the Group. But I hardly need remind you that your brother, Rodolfo Spada, after leaving the Group with a slamming of the door which will have historical resonance, has fled to a secret locality in *Venetia.*"

"Dear Signor Boldrin, I seem to gather from your talk that you and my brother are somehow implicated in plans for the kidnaping of I don't know which eminent persons who occupy, as you rather curiously put it, vice-presidential positions. I wish to make it perfectly clear to you that any kind of folly on the part of my brother wouldn't surprise me. And I have already told you what my position is: while opposing the death penalty, I would favor life imprisonment for the planners and executors of such enterprises, or a criminal lunatic asylum, also for life. In the case of my brother I might say that practically since he was born I've been suggesting the lunatic asylum, period. The Rodolfo file, as far as I am concerned, has been and continues to be definitively shelved. Would you like a drop of wine?"

The two ladies serve wine to everybody. Boldrin grabs his glass without turning his eyes away from the ambassador, as if hypnotized.

Piglioli-Spada takes a swallow of wine with visible delight and goes on: "Lately here we've been busy with an affair which I know does not involve you. My niece—my brother's daughter, as it happens—has disappeared." He produces a cunning little smile as if he feels he has somehow trapped Boldrin. "I do not believe there is a kidnaping to begin with. I would describe a kidnaping as the seizure of an unconsenting person. In our case there must have been full consent on the part of the seized person, and you'll permit me to pass over the reasons for my conviction."

"Your niece has disappeared? But I came here to look for her."

"You are not the only one. You are all confused travelers, as it were." The ambassador's manner becomes arrogant, amused and spiteful. "You journalists most especially. You never know anything. You came here with the declared intention of speaking to my brother, who, if the family have a minimum of common sense, will have to be declared legally incompetent. As to his wife, my sister-in-law, Maria Laura, I'd rather not mention her. She, and a lady friend, who incidentally strikes me as rather shady, take a trip together every year in the spring. Who knows where they are now?"

Here Boldrin's stupefied look suddenly changes, first becoming ironical, then sharp and calculating. "Right," he says, "who knows where the two ladies are?"

Then something happens, which Boldrin interprets as a definite gift from Fate: Bice and Flora look at the clock. It is time for a television program they never miss, and shortly thereafter the ambassador gets up too. Since he has been conducting the search for his niece, he has regained vitality, eloquence, an identity, a certain delight in living. He has resumed a habit of staying on in the room downstairs after his wife, ill since time immemorial, has retired to rest, but he goes up to see her a couple of times before starting to go to bed himself.

Alone with his two contemporaries, Molisani and Brunetti, Boldrin points to the door through which the ambassador has just gone out: "I imagine you have by now realized that this man is insane."

The two young men produce little spurts of laughter, amused, curious. Boldrin asks peremptorily, "Where did you put the girl?"

The two young men go on giggling; they say they know even less than he does.

Boldrin, with authority: "Why did you boys stay on here?"

"I had nothing better to do; I brought Brunetti here today and they've already asked him to stay. It's comfortable and those two ladies upstairs are marvelous cooks."

Brunetti shrugs and smiles. "I am an unpaid assistant at

the university, in international law, and our department is inactive on account of a sit-in. What would you do, Boldrin, if you were in my place?"

"I would leave. We'll go. We'll immediately abandon this lunatic. We'll go up to Venetia, to look for his brother. He has retired in Venetia, the region that calls the tune in Italy." His head is thrust forward like a catapult and his wide blue gaze wanders over the two young men while his speech proceeds like a cataract:

"The Group performs activities in Venice which I shall limit myself to describe as investigative, under various pseudo-cultural labels—pseudo-religious, pseudo-ecological, et cetera; all very fashionable." Boldrin raises his head, and like a dog barking to the sky he bursts into long, solitary laughter, then he turns frightfully serious again, his blue eyes scintillating. "Well, then, in the same way as preventive searches are conducted in houses designated to be the official residences of illustrious visitors, or as the foods destined to them are scrupulously examined, analyzed, filtered, so any written line, any expressed opinion, any syllable we may have pronounced on the subject of any prominent Vice-President will be examined down to the hundredth of an inch, and nothing will be easier than to turn their contents and tenor against us.

"It will therefore be easy for the electronic computer, a Methuselah with a memory spreading over the millennia, which keeps in storage all of our writings and thoughts and can recall them totally in one millionth of a second—it will indeed be very easy for him to produce electronic emissions which, once decoded by the operators, will transform themselves into threatening alliterative charges against us: inept intellectuals, malevolent maladjusted minds, destructive dissent, serpentine subterrenean subversion. Do we understand each other, Brunetti?"

"I can't say I understand you well, but you are extremely entertaining. I agree, we'll all go up to Venetia. Right?"

Molisani, rather resembling a huge timid lamb: "So we abandon Signor Camillo just like that?"

Boldrin instructs them: "When the ambassador comes down, I'll take my leave. He'll be only too happy to see me go. I'll say that sometimes I have trouble starting my car, and that if that should happen I'd honk three times so you can come out and give me a push. How many cars do you have?"

"One, my own car which is now in that kind of little church."

"You'll follow me in your car until Rovigo or Padua, where I know everybody, and there we'll all get into my car and go on to the master's hiding place."

The ambassador offers Boldrin one last glass of wine before wishing him a nice trip and dismissing him. In a short while, the three honks resound in the darkness. It is also beginning to rain.

Waiting for Molisani and Brunetti to come back in, the ambassador pours himself more wine and on that he dozes off. When he wakes up, the rain is pouring. At this point in his life there is nothing but the noise of pouring rain. His head is empty. When thought slowly begins to circulate in it again, he charges out through the front door into the driving rain. He runs into the garage-chapel—deserted. In here too there are showers of rain through the roof. In his loneliness and hallucination, he lets the water run down his white hair, his face. Then he believes he's seeing his son, Amedeo, as a faint ghost. The little chapel was still functioning, then. Although the funeral was not held here, a mass was celebrated on the thirtieth day after the death, the *trigesimo*.

XIX

Rodolfo Spada:

I'll summarize. The day before yesterday, in the morning, I received a distinct telepathic signal. I was sitting at my desk; in the first light of the sun the flowers which the Spadone twins and my daughter always arrange for me were already in perfect focus, like a very lucid thought.

The night before, at dinner, during one of his usual verbal floods, Remigio Ferro had said to me, "Daphne sends you greetings. She's still in Lugano but in a few days she'll go to Venice. She called to tell me . . ."

Evidently I must have ceased to pay attention to him at that point; in fact, I suppose I was never fully listening to him, but the next morning, standing in front of the flowers in the early sunlight, I found his words registered in my brain and rushed up to the room where Remigio Ferro works. My apparent motive was to ask him to repeat what he had said about Daphne, but I immediately recognized the real one. I found Remigio dictating to an unknown young lady, slender, brown-haired, who received me smiling, with an expression of total and absolute certainty in her wide, clear, direct eyes. I mean that from the first moment there was the kind of surprise that is equal to recognition. It didn't even vaguely occur to me to reproach Remigio for having brought an absolute stranger here without my permission: it was clear at once that the person had not come to him but to me and that she was instantly becoming very well known.

"This is Diana, my new secretary," Ferro announced. "She's just arrived from Switzerland and I'm already dictating a script to her. We'll all be in it. Diana is excellent. She was sent to me by your old friend Daphne." These completely irrelevant words drifted along without leaving any mark. Diana and I were looking at each other without the slightest doubt or uncertainty.

She has lived in the Swiss-Italian region, Ticino, and speaks with a Lombard accent. Daughter of a teacher, she grew up among memories of Italian political exiles of the Risorgimento. We spoke of Cattaneo and others while I took her walking through fields and boating over these vast green waters. Here as we lay on the bottom of the boat she scrutinized my eyes and said, "I hadn't realized it at first: your eyes are very light."

"It must be you that changed them." I abandoned myself to a digression: "At Succaso we had a record with a portrait of Brahms on the jacket, in color. I would like to be like him. Like Brahms. Flowing silver beard, freshly laundered skin, cool pale blue eyes. Sky and milk, but at the same time, mind you, massively solid. A massively solid dream. Rocklike and evanescent at the same time. Whereas my steel-wire jockey physique, as I would tell myself, and my coal-black eyes are those of a man hunted, an outcast, a conspirator."

"No, your eyes are bright and clear. The water around here is still clear too."

She mentioned the kind of work she did for Daphne, collecting publications and data on ecology: air and water (which here around us happen to be still alive and well) infected by now nearly everywhere, poison spreading like an oil stain. Mercury used in a factory pollutes sea water so that men and animals either die or will live on in a state of permanent tremor. Piercing noise from machinery of the building industry causes miscarriages in pregnant women.

I told Diana that after discussing a given subject, the boys and girls here compose a "memo" which is then transcribed in paint on large sheets of paper and posted by Luigi and the others on the façades of public buildings and schools.

Ordinary goldfish dropped in water close to industrial waste die within ten minutes. Smell in the air: between putrid and sulfurous. Animals and birds float along in a stupor, then they are washed ashore, dead. Only living thing: the worm, feeding on decomposing garbage. In the vegetable gardens, big beautiful tomatoes are all rotten inside.

Diana says, "These would be Daphne's subjects, but the things she reads never sound real."

"Right. I knew Daphne at a time when she lived in total reality but later she got lost in committees for salvage operations when such matters became socially and politically fashionable; I only need to mention that even the Group is getting involved in such things, and it will immediately be clear that the very idea of saving life is falling like everything else into the hands of people outside of reality."

She asked me, "Why do you all treat me so well? I feel as though I had always known Vittorino, the Spadone twins, Luigi . . ."

"Luigi is a young man of genius, very quick in his mind and also in his physical motions, having legs so long that they seem to bifurcate at his chest. Though he was thrown out of the Brusò school, he's excellent, especially in the natural sciences. He constantly reads books on entomology and such. He would study genetics at the university if ever one day they accept him, which is highly improbable. Even as a child he was corresponding with butterfly collectors in Texas or Thailand. Physical and mental destructions go on undeterred, but the Luigis, scattered all over the world, go on sending each other information on tiny little flying beings, insect legs microphotographed, magnified wings looking like silver sails with fanciful filigrees. Governments don't even vaguely know the voters of tomorrow, the clarity and cheerfulness of their minds, the nonchalant amplitude of their curiosities. Suddenly the morning of revelations will dawn, and the governmental candidates will be caught, unprepared and stupefied, entirely out of the game."

From the way her intent hazel eyes stare at me, one might suspect that Diana and I are in danger of becoming Twin Souls. Nothing could be less desirable. But even on this point we understand each other without saying a word. If I start preaching a little, she laughs at me. And considering that we are now alone on the terrace at sunset in front of trees which give us back our shadows disproportionately enlarged yet wholly individualized, first I caress her beautiful face, then we fall into each other's arms and our shapes mingle in the thick of the trees.

Later in the night she resumes her motif: "You have clear eyes. And who's pursuing you? Even so, you could always escape with me."

For two days she brought us up to the mountains as if we were already looking for possible Alpine escape routes in case of danger. I have already made it clear that nature descriptions are not for me, so imagine if I want to try the most boring variety within that genre, namely the description of mountain landscapes. Everything was very adequately savored but in silence, the crystal quality of the rocks and the air, the lively punctures of sunlight through the pine trees, the excellent grappa, and so forth. And the walks down green slopes, like flying.

There were the usual young people and their friends who, I realize, are increasing in number; as the community grows, by synergism its intelligence and cheerfulness grow too. One of the Spadone twins was missing, having gone to Venice. I have noticed that I cannot yet tell the two girls apart; but clearly the Spadone we had with us was not the guitar player, though she was coupled with a young man who in turn had come from Venice. Up in the mountains they sang casually, without accompanying instruments. I even enjoyed some Alpine war songs which I had previously found obnoxious because they reminded me of my father in his phony soldier capacity.

To solve my doubts on their identities, the Spadone girl who was with us said gently to me, "We have very simple names, you know; she is Ginetta and I am Margherita. And *his* name"—pointing to the young man who held her strongly by the waist—"is Benn." Then, purring in Benn's arms, she went on in a rambling autobiographical vein: "The countess sometimes says that we are her granddaughters, that is, daughters of one of her sons dead on the battlefield. But at other times she says that actually our father was her cousin Diomede, the one who died in a motorcycle accident."

Diana later told me, "I knew their names and I can tell them apart very well. Ginetta, in Venice, will see Daphne."

"I know. She rushed there, I presume, to save the city."

Diana shrugs; her motions remind me of my daughter. I embrace her with continuous and total joy; who knows whether such happiness is really deserved?

Young Benn, now twined around Margherita Spadone, is described as an American, though he actually lives in Venice; he informs me that as of this moment his father, Josiah C. Benn, is in Venice, too, and knows me by reputation. The young man laughs obstreperously as he offers these data, so totally irrelevant and unreal to both of us. It seems that his father, who is half Italian and half German but has been an American for several decades, is an eminent figure in the Group, adorned with a very impressive title, like "international inspector." Young Benn, unlike his father, operates within a human dimension and is in love with Margherita Spadone, who, being an excellent cook and lover, returns his attentions with complete and lively gracefulness, making him blissfully happy. Young Benn had never dreamed that life could be so simple and agreeable.

Diana told me that Daphne is now very well and this gives me joy. Daphne has a very complicated clinical record; years ago I spent long, pained days by her bed where she was suffering physically and psychologically. Diana has heard tales about my violent love affair with Daphne, but they haven't touched her. Actually, from the very first exchange of looks there has been mutually perfect focus between Diana and myself, a state I never reached with Daphne even during our supreme moments. I haven't the slightest doubt. Our life here consists of making continuous discoveries, ever more lucid, important and enjoyable, even in the area of mutual affections. I'll hasten to add that after this I won't say anything more. If I am not in favor of nature descriptions, imagine how I feel about descriptions of love scenes, which are generally animated by two forms of sickness that are alien to me, exhibitionism at one end and voyeurism at the other.

·   ·   ·

I resume. I might as well write down at once about the hullabaloo of last night. Remigio Ferro was very jealous because Ginetta had not yet returned. Ferro always feels the urge to put on a scene of some sort, in which he assigns an important role to himself to be acted with inebriated verbosity. "Where's the other twin? What is she doing? I want to know it minute by minute even if it should make me suffer." The rest of us were already in our rooms, and he wandered from one to the other to describe his feelings.

The sound of an automobile was heard approaching, stopping at our house. Ferro rushed to the window, he saw headlights in the dark; then the man who had been driving came out of the car, or rather it was the shadow of a man, not tall, sturdy, wearing a dark suit. Before closing the door, this shadow bent over to talk to someone who had remained in the car. Then he walked with determination to the front door of our house.

Ferro immediately grabbed this chance to put on a new scene: "That fellow has the classic look of the plain-clothes man. This is it, they're here to catch me, I feel it." He was going to rush downstairs, his arms thrust forward, as if offering his wrists to be handcuffed, but I stopped him, holding him by the wrist in *my* iron grip. The old hammer bell of this dear rusty house resounded long and vigorously. I held back everybody except Diana, asking her to go to the window and order the man to identify himself. Actually Diana was preparing to do just that. I stood behind her with a gun, ready if necessary, to fire, a few shots by way of warning.

A voice well known to me replied to Diana's question: "We are three friends who have come to greet Rodolfo Spada. If you insist I can tell you my name, though I'm sure the name is entirely unknown and irrelevant to you. I am Diego Boldrin."

I fired one shot, just as an appetizer, against the night sky. Meanwhile Vittorino rushed to the window. "Look," he said to the newcomer, "Professor Spada is not here; he has left, *perhaps* for Babiana Terme, perhaps someplace much farther away."

"Who are you? And why did you fire that shot?"

I saw no reason to frighten Boldrin without necessity, so I asked Diana to go downstairs and with sober kindness exhort the young man to leave. I very much hope that Boldrin may salvage that large head of his, with the thoughts and visions it contains, but he must do that all by himself. From on high, Vittorino and I watched the scene as from a theater gallery.

Two new figures emerged from the car. I recognized one of the two: Molisani. The other's face was not new to me either, but I didn't know who he was. Both young, with a beard apiece.

Ferro insisted on going down too, and my daughter accompanied him to keep an eye on him and prevent his useless histrionic outbursts. I must say that later on Ferro's actions proved very effective. He has moments when his maniacal personality carries him to the threshold of genius. I had always regarded him as an acquaintance, but lately I have seen in him, much to my satisfaction, a friend.

When Boldrin saw my daughter appear he started howling. It seems that he was looking for her rather than for me. I can't blame him. Meanwhile she and Molisani were falling into each other's arms exchanging long kisses. Then she and the other young man kissed each other's cheeks. Both she and Diana advised the three young men to go and look for a place to sleep at a Brusò inn, unless they wanted to leave immediately for places farther away.

A long confabulation among them followed. Then Vittorino sent one of his strong, throaty whispers through the night air: "Silence, the countess is asleep."

Boldrin looked up blindly: "Who are you? Which countess?"

"My grandmother. I'm the count. The one dead in the war, not the one dead on the motorcycle. Count Spadone."

I heard Boldrin's softened voice: "Poor boy, that must be Fornasier's son, the one who is slightly demented."

Boldrin insisted on finding out from Diana and my daughter where I was, and again Vittorino cut in from above: "He's been away for quite a while now. I don't promise anything, but look for him at Babiana Terme. He may have gone to Switzerland instead, escaped across the border, you know?"

Boldrin then simply asked for permission to come in and make a phone call. "Not possible. We have no telephone." To get things moving, Ferro suggested that Boldrin get into my car; the other two young men followed them in their car; Diana and my daughter got into this second car too.

These two dear girls came back an hour later, with Ferro; it isn't clear where the three young men went, perhaps to Venice. There was no room at the inn; Boldrin was only allowed to use the telephone. Curious thing: first of all, he wanted to call Succaso. My daughter suggested that it would be stupidly cruel to wake up Uncle Camillo and Aunt Adele. She asked disinterestedly why Boldrin wanted to call Succaso, but the good boy took on an air of mystery. Then, as my dear young ladies reported to me, he put in an even stranger call to a hotel on the Ionian Sea, asking to talk with either my wife or Professor Matilde Apicetta.

Here Diana and my daughter, who actually resemble each

other a little, look caressingly at me, trying to arouse my curiosity. To make them happy, I ask, "And what did he talk about, with Laura and Matilde?"

"About nothing, because they told him that the two ladies were no longer there; they told him the two ladies had left for America."

We burst out laughing, rather to express our continuous state of well-being then to comment on the specific situation. And it goes without saying that the relations between Boldrin and Succaso are just as uninteresting to us. Frankly, I forgot to ask myself any questions about what Camillo might be doing.

In the end, there was Ferro's triumph. He told us about it himself, repeating his story several times: "There were no rooms at the inn, so I took Boldrin aside, looked him straight in the eye and told him, 'Look, Boldrin: Rodolfo Spada has resumed his flight; searching for him would be useless and inadvisable; and at any rate, your subconscious aspiration is to identify with the master by somehow getting to possess one of his women. Now, Genzianella and Diana will stay on here, Laura is in America, you have only Daphne left. She is in Venice. Your city. Go and look for Daphne in Venice. She will give new meaning to your life.' Well, I hypnotized him. He understood me. Life will imitate my improvised inventions." He concludes: "And then, I like Boldrin because he is a hothead, a fanatic."

At the peak, toward dawn, Ginetta came back, brought by somebody on a motorcycle. Very affectionate toward Ferro, who held her in his arms and kept saying, "Don't tell me where you've been or what you've done. Don't ever tell me anything. Only, from now on, don't ever leave me."

No one felt like going to sleep any more, and at the perfectly right moment Countess Spadone arrived and took us to her house through sparkling green fields of grass. The boys and girls go to her house quite often; and then the atmosphere, I would say, is characterized by foam—from wine, and from shampoo; she offers a very pleasurable sparkling wine, and she washes everybody's hair. She is the one who invents the twins' hairdos, always so fanciful and festive.

She has been practicing these activities from time immemorial, and she explains to me: "During one of the difficult periods I worked as a hairdresser, here, in our villages; no one beats me in producing fluffy hair, grass in the summer sun, you know, nature? I keep Vittorino's hair short because he likes to swim, or sit on a tree, and there is so much wind, but look, feel, what soft fur. The twins come to me to make themselves beautiful because I have the most marvelous bathroom in Venetia, old marble, copper furnace, wonderful steam from water heated on wood fire, oh!

"You have followed the right instinct, Rudolph, coming here from central Italy, where they treated you roughly. No, I know nothing, don't say anything. I am not a sorceress, I don't read the cards, and then, I don't have culture like you —only, I know that here you become whole. In peace. So do your daughter and Diana and your friend Ferro, who is very sweet and who needed this so badly after a life of beatings, oh!

"Freedom and peace, Rudolph, and peace doesn't at all mean emptiness and torpor. Ridiculous! It means the development of feelings, inebriations too, being whole, not stunted!

"In the Venetian region I am acquainted with the highest-ranking people, and I know that with what they possess and accumulate they could live for as long as they please the way you live, with trifling expenditures, in our ancient villa; but instead, they must continue the merry-go-round, don't they? And deep inside they're all so very, very bored, also the ones with the highest salaries, you know? And then, so very sad. Their sickness is that they continuously desire to see themselves on TV, though they're ugly, dull, with hair slicked down with oil."

She went on rambling for over an hour, washing everybody's hair while the sun rose and Vittorino, Diana and my daughter were pouring wine.

"One of these high-ranking people was at a hotel in Babiana, where the bathrooms are horrid, and he asked me who you were, he wanted the formula of how you all live, which is the way I too have always lived; but you can't answer, because when you talk to one of them, he isn't really there in front of you, whole; he is scattered about, one piece here, another piece there, and although he's so fragmented he's always full of occupations, always in an automobile. Puppets!"

After having washed and combed all of the boys and girls she touched their hair proudly; in the end she toasted them, with much vivacity, in the cascading sunlight: "They are handsome, very young, very amorous, and they won't die the way their fathers had to die for the fatherland and fall back on religion, military chaplains, you know? Oh, these young people here will see the year 2000, the year 2050 and perhaps 2100, because by then living much more than a hundred years won't surprise anybody."

XX

Ugo Crocetti Vidal, Benito Giuseppe's father, became an American a quarter century ago here in Manhattan and on that occasion, after he had filled out many forms and questionnaires, he was given a card with a line on which he was to write the name he had borne until then, and another line on which he could write the name he might want to be called from then on; in other words, he was casually being invited to choose a new identity for himself. For some time Ugo Crocetti had found his double surname too cumbersome, so first of all he dropped "Vidal," then sanctioned the English pronunciation of "Crocetti" by deciding to become Mr. Crossetti. And he added a final little touch to his Christian name.

At that time Hugo Crossetti was already occupying the spacious old apartment in the Atlantic metropolis where he lives today. At this moment, twenty-five years later, in the almost unchanged living room with its majestic furniture, high ceilings, heavy canopylike curtains on doors and windows, seated on the edge of a silk-covered sofa with floral gold embroideries, leaning over the vast low table with its dark marble top, his arms thrust forward, his hands hanging over a huge marble ashtray as over a holy-water basin, Hugo

Crossetti is lovingly cutting his fingernails with a pair of small golden scissors. Fragments shaped like minuscule new moons fall into the immense ashtray.

This occupation absorbs and delights him. Hugo Crossetti's life is an embroidery of continuous and diverse joys, savored in depth—from brief happy ceremonies like the bi-weekly cutting of his fingernails, to solemn yearly ones like the Holy Mass, sumptuous and deeply moving, which he orders every year on the anniversary of the death of Benito Giuseppe's mother. After the death of that first wife, whom he left back in Italy with Benito Giuseppe, then an infant, Hugo Crossetti married twice but had no other children, and both new marriages ended in divorce.

Grown rich by his skill in plastics, Hugo hasn't a single ounce of such materials in his house because the house to him is Art, Beauty, the Renaissance. He says: "Everything in my house is done so that a woman in it may feel like a queen." Fifty-two and affluent, he has slowed up his working pace so that his state of preservation seems better every day. His hair is black and strong, parted in the middle and thrown back fan-wise, immobilized by brilliantine. The central theme in his life now is his rapport with women, and the calm, full, well-regulated enjoyment of that rapport. He reads little but in depth, he is hospitable, he keeps in touch with well-informed people. He considers himself a good student of the Bible. He is an expert on riddles and puzzles. He is a member of reading groups and of small, exclusive amateur acting companies. He is secretary-treasurer of the Leonardo da Vinci Cultural Association.

The first words spoken to him by Laura Piglioli-Spada, there on a visit with Matilde Apicetta, were: "In Italy I haven't seen men like you since I was a child, if indeed there were any—perhaps my father in some ways. Benito Giuseppe doesn't look like you, maybe Elio does, your nephew." Then, dreamily, her mind bouncing back to the Ionian Sea, seeing with affection her own naked breast with Elio Vidal's large, protective, hairy hand lying on it: "Even Elio doesn't look very much like you, though."

"I don't know much about Elio. But my own boy, Benito Giuseppe, that's the brain of the clan. He has very progressive ideas, you know. In 1940 I wanted to get them over here, he and his mother, but the war came and then everything—"

Matilde Apicetta interrupts: "They were not wanted, and for that matter, neither of the two would have come, and you know this very well, Hugo."

Arriving at the airport, Matilde and Laura had been pushed around by the crowd and were awed by the immigration officials seated in their glass cubicles standing on lineoleum floors; besides, Laura couldn't find her vaccination certificate and had to be revaccinated. Under the fluorescent light, her round arm seemed made of plastic. Then they were suffocated by the heat and by high piles of luggage; at customs inspection the most familiar objects, night gowns, stockings, erupting from their suitcases, looked like falsifications in that light. Up high, behind thick glass partitions that excluded all outside sounds, they saw a huge crowd waiting.

For two hours Hugo Crossetti was an indistinguishable fragment in that mass. Up there behind glass, insulated, for two hours he held his black fedora in his hand and smilingly caressed the flower on his lapel, the recognition signal for the two ladies whom he prefigured as very beautiful.

After passing through customs, they were suddenly free, abandoned to themselves as in a desert, in spite of the crowd: a crowd of people who didn't look at anyone, many of the men not wearing neckties, some with psychedelic shirts and embroidered pants. The two women laughed nervously: "There isn't a single man that may remotely be taken to be Peppino Crocetti Vidal's father. And anyway, we don't even remember whether Elio said red flower or red umbrella."

Among the lacerating noises continuously emitted by the loudspeakers there suddenly erupted the sound of their own names. They felt themselves transformed into artificial images, the same as had happened to their underwear in the wide-open suitcases. The order was to go to a special waiting room for privileged travelers. Here they found Hugo Crossetti, holding his right-hand glove in his gloved left hand, proffering his bare right hand to greet them. They immediately started drinking excellent whiskey.

Hugo brought them into the city in a large, old-fashioned, extremely soft automobile, black and gold, with a driver in matching colors, and curtained windows. They caught fragmentary glimpses of a gray, barren, neon-lit countryside, then of interminably tall buildings, with thousands of windows; they turned their eyes away to the car's interior, to the curtains, to the heavy silken cords with tassels, to the crystal flower vases, and to the roseate, silent-film handsome face of Hugo Crossetti.

For the first forty-eight hours of the two ladies' visit Hugo had already lined up a half-dozen invitations from some of his friends; so they got to know a hidden city, old and slow, with hyperdecorated living rooms and gentlemen of his same age but with grayer hair, full of attentions, of kindness, of mannerisms. Laura enchanted them, she always ended up holding hands and interlacing fingers with one or the other of them when after dinner they sank in deep sofas sipping espresso and liqueurs. The ladies found everything very comfortable and relaxing, including their rooms in Hugo's house with beds and velvet-covered chaise longues, tall mirrors and old clocks, bathrooms with marble, brass, mother-of-pearl.

This evening Hugo is giving a little dinner party for eight in his home. Three of the gentlemen they had met in previous evenings are already present: one is there with his wife; another, a professor, is paired with Matilde; while it is tacitly acknowledged that Hugo is paired with Laura; so only one lady is missing yet, and she has been announced by Hugo as the *pièce de résistance* of the evening, a journalist who finally arrives, independent and very late, and starts talking immediately; she is very tall, dark-haired, bilingual, and her name is Perla Manzoni.

"Here she is, this is Perla Manzoni," Hugo announces radiantly. "She doesn't work for the, uh, well-known Group but for another group, and several European periodicals have published an interview which she conducted in a secret location with a subterranean young man whom she refuses to identify—uh uh, not even his initials—who is the brain of the so-called vice squad that is a subterranean intercontinental association specializing in the kidnaping of vice-people."

"What vice?"

"Vice."

"Vice-somebody."

"Not only Vice-Presidents but also vice-secretaries of government agencies, of political parties, a little bit of everything."

The professor especially and all the others except Laura smile knowingly as they listen to Perla Manzoni, who in turn has listened directly to the organizer of these original kidnapings. It is impossible for Laura to unravel the tangle of questions and answers which cross the air and melt into one another:

"It looks like a curious idea but it is very logical."

"French and German papers too?"

"And what does he look like?"

"In Italy too."

"He is an executor. Men have no time to think, so it's up to us women to do the thinking for them; in other words, we carry on the business of history, in the sense of active and militant thought."

"I was the first to interview him and I assure you he has neither long hair nor a beard."

"The complex is on the Ionian Sea, a sea which is filled with poetry."

"A very handsome boy, blond and pink, with tortoise-rimmed glasses, dressed and combed like those young Englishmen who were usually called Peter or Christopher."

"It isn't this group, it's the other group."

"One of the centers is in Venetia."

"Venetia too is filled with poetry."

"Which group?"

None of these eight people have heard the apartment bell ring. A butler hired for the evening, older than any of the guests, steals out silently and comes back with a telegram on a silver plate; he gives it to Hugo but it is addressed to *Marialaura Pigliolispada c/o Crocetti,* so Hugo nods at the butler who passes it on to Laura. Laura opens the telegram and lip-reads the contents; no one watches her; everybody talks; Hugo is following a dialogue on economic policy between the professor and Matilde.

Laura hands the telegram to Matilde who reads it out loud: "YOUR FRIEND DAPHNE INFORMS YOUR PRESENT WHEREABOUTS STOP YOUR DAUGHTER DISAPPEARED STOP AFTER THOROUGH ANALYSIS SITUATION AM RENOUNCING SURVEILLANCE TASK ALSO SUSPENDING FURTHER SEARCH STOP CORDIALLY CAMILLO."

Matilde suggests that they call Daphne on the phone; Hugo is immediately on his feet and gets the name of the Venice hotel where Daphne is now; with a golden pencil he marks it in a leatherbound notebook and goes to the telephone in a corner of the room. The telephone, carefully selected by Hugo in an antique appliances shop, is gold and black with a pedestal shaped like that of an equestrian monument, the receiver occupying the place of the bronze warrior on horseback.

The streams of conversation continue to run before Laura's blue-green eyes, with some new motifs:

"Who is Daphne?"

"The financing of the complex."

"They study problems in depth; sexology will take giant steps forward."

Hugo, coming back to sit among his friends, radiates hospitality and satisfaction. The phone rings, Hugo raises a forefinger: "Here she is." Laura follows him to the phone. With a wide smile full of health, Hugo offers her the receiver and places near her, on the mahogany table, a note pad of precious Fabriano paper, a red pen and a glass of port.

"This is Laura. Can you hear me? Daphne?"

From Venice through outer space an astral but acute voice carries neat and well-articulated words: "I hear you very well and I do not dare suppose that my voice may stir any significant reverberation in you, perhaps not even my name, in spite of a recent encounter. I am Diego Boldrin."

"Boldrin dear, I am speaking from America; may I talk to Daphne?"

"Signora Spada, I am speaking from the living room in Daphne's suite; Daphne is in the bedroom and has given orders not to be awakened."

"No. I'm here." An unmistakable husky voice, clearly from the bed.

"Daphne dear, I've just received a telegram from my brother-in-law who says that Genzianella has disappeared and that he, Camillo, doesn't care. Where has she disappeared?"

"Signora Spada, I have seen your daughter quite recently; in its very different way, her appearance is as impressive as that of Daphne here."

"Your daughter is all right, but apparently Rodolfo has disappeared again."

"Signora, the Fornasier boy, the one who is slightly demented, has hinted at a possible escape to Switzerland. The atmosphere is heavy"—Boldrin's electronically filtered voice sounds penetrating and bemused—"we are all on police files; Ferro, the film director, is here under a false name and is preparing a script on the vice-presidential kidnaping."

"What's the meaning of all this, Boldrin?"

"Does it escape you, Signora Spada? Don't you perceive the wonderful irony in the very idea of kidnaping a vice-person? The Chief, be he President or whatever, will be compelled to waste time and energy on this pallid echo man, this shadow man who would be easily replaceable but, once kidnaped, jumps to the forefront, steals the headlines, the limelight, the centrality of the image, compelling the Chief to organize searches and press conferences publicizing no longer himself but the other one, the shadow . . ."

"Look, Boldrin, as usual I don't understand much of what you're saying; besides, it seems to me that here too, in Hugo's living room, they were talking about some of the same things you mention, and the coincidence is slightly nightmarish, I find. But tell me again, where is Rodolfo?"

"The pressures of the moment may have compelled him

to find a new refuge. The Group is vigilant and does not forgive. Observe that I am not saying B.G.C.V., I'm saying the Group. It seems that the highly important Josiah C. Benn is in Venice at the moment, where the Group has bought a dogal residence for a mere pittance. Hello?"

"I'm here, Boldrin dear, but as I told you, I never understand you very well. Try and keep Daphne awake, please, till she can answer me. You all do love my husband, don't you? Well, then, you must always remember that Rodolfo is not quite sound mentally. Hello? Hello?"

There has been something like an electric discharge, followed by a sound as of ocean waves tuned down to a whisper. *Boldrin has hung up on her.*

"Anyway, I never understand Boldrin, and Daphne was in a coma. At this point, I find, you Matilde should call Peppino Crocetti Vidal in Rome."

"Boldrin is a scatterbrain, poor boy. Hugo, may we use your phone to call Peppino in Rome?"

Hugo Crossetti radiates a kind of quiet inebriety, not so much at the idea of calling his son in Rome as at the idea of coming to the ladies' assistance by providing new transatlantic calls from his house full of technological resources hidden in the folds of Art.

This time Matilde goes to the monumental telephone; it's 7 A.M. in Rome, and Crocetti Vidal has just awakened, his golden voice is harmonious and clear: "Our young friend Boldrin, who had been charged with a fact-finding mission to our Ionian complex, unexpectedly called me from Venice. With his talk he seemed to suggest, in substance, that we consult with our European and American associates for the eventual definition of a common attitude in regard to the Remigio Ferro case as well as to the Rodolfo Spada case."

"Are you referring to Ferro's troubles on account of his

motion picture? The scandal with the young girls? What does Rodolfo have to do with that?"

"The two cases are separate in spite of our two friends' recent cohabitation in the same locality, which as you know is the Fornasier estate at Brusò. And besides, the configuration of both cases seems qualified by the fact that a son of our friend Benn is at Brusò. His particular position as a father clearly constitutes a motivational element in Benn's concern with events there."

"Which events? And have you any idea where Rodolfo may be now?"

"Both Ferro and Spada seem to have disappeared; I don't know whether their disappearance should be classified as an escape. Among several suspended options, I would suggest that you give highest priority to your speedy return here. Did you find a hospital for Spada?"

Laura, with Hugo beside her, had been listening on the bedroom extension. She hangs up. "And I so wanted to see the new museums," she says quietly.

Later she and Hugo are in that same room, all guests long gone, the suitcases ready. Hugo came to seek her in the night, wearing a robe seemingly cut out of a piece of tapestry with golden trimmings; everything between the two of them has happened in perfect silence, the slow preparation, the long caresses and finally love, from which Laura has directly slid into sleep.

Only after love and sleep has she started to talk; in fact, she has been awakened by her own voice shouting: "Rodolfo, what are you doing here?" Then, awake, but still entangled in sleep: "Oh, no, he has fled again; you heard that too, didn't you, that he has fled again?" Addressing taciturn Hugo, she has tried to explain everything: "The same happened with your cousin, Elio, or whatever he is, your nephew; and with others before him. I find myself in their arms, they hold me tight, they do anything they please with me, yet at some point they must realize that it is as if I weren't there any more. That's the moment when I have a dream, always the same: I see myself navigating on a smooth golden sea, with Rodolfo. There used to be so much vigor in that little sailor, in that magnificent jockey made of steel. Rodolfo and I were the same size, strong, small, handsome. What an injustice, after all, his maniacal retirement, his folly. Dalle Noci has examined him, there's nothing too alarming, but I believe he'll never recover. Always with something to hide, looking like a petty thief, or rather, like a child, who believes nobody notices his filching. Secret thoughts. Many years ago he found Daphne, a friend of mine, and I told myself: I have no right to be jealous; in fact, I'm happy if he finds a little pleasure in her. Daphne was very beautiful then, very experienced. I didn't interest them any more, I was a perfectly healthy apple. Let him freely take his pleasure. I would go away on these long trips with Matilde, we manage to take them practically without spending a penny. This time it's the Group, Vidal, things like that. I liked your son very much when I saw him but he is isolated, inaccessible. Elio is exuberant, a force of nature, we made love even in that room with the toy trains, and in the helicopter, but it's all the same. I am looking for somebody who may really subjugate me. Vladonicic, he was enormous, but you should have seen! I daresay a woman could do better. Matilde. Or Daphne herself. But they are always so busy, also frequently ill. I never catch anything, not even a cold, so they drop me. Being ill is a way to participate in life. Daphne has undergone sleep therapy, also electroshock several times. She's interested in everything, like Matilde and even more, so she always has something to talk about, like that Perla Manzoni. Certainly Daphne has had various husbands who have financed her activities, her illnesses too. In a few hours Matilde and I will fly back. Thanks for everything, embrace me again if you want. We owe this trip to Elio Vidal, to the Group, ultimately to Peppino, even though at first he had no idea we'd end up here. Curious thing, now I speak of him as if he were a stranger, though he is your son. There's always someone that makes things easy for us, and besides, Matilde is involved in so many activities. I am always happy, except for this thought I have, wanting to be subjected to somebody, and never managing to."

Hugo Crossetti is vanquished, embittered, he smiles wanly. But to him every woman is a queen, so after a last embrace he gets up and orders the monumental car to accompany the two ladies to the airport.

XXI

Diego Boldrin:

I have enough self-knowledge and sense of responsibility to be able to say clearly to my conscience that whatever I do, I do in order to amuse myself. True, I am always on the ball, twenty-four hours out of twenty-four, a preacher, a missionary of reportage, attacking anybody, anywhere, with my continuous flow of words; but I can always perceive within myself this excited and sinful feeling of amusement.

Venice, my native city, is the center of the world, and Dorsoduro is the nerve center of Venice. Former schoolmates of mine live here and I meet them in the gardens of restaurants. They keep me informed about the city from which, for reasons connected with my work, I am always away. Many resident or transient foreigners also come to these gardens; among them Daphne, who gave me an appointment here through the mediation of Ferro. Here Venetians and foreigners all know each other and talk by phone or meet as much as several times a day.

Meeting with Daphne. I was sitting in the garden with my old schoolmate Camentini. He used to be timid but he later became an opposition extremist. He led night missions against the excavation machinery with which big industry is ruining the Venetian lagoon, and he has organized forays of mass destruction on the nefarious pigeons, whose excrement contributes to the death of bronzes and marbles. It seems that he is also connected with the "vice squads" but this is not certain because lately his manner has become darker, he tells you the simplest things with an air of mystery. His first words to me are, "I've just come back from Milan; I was there for two days," and he holds his firm, heavy eyes fixed on me as though he were saying, "I've had a final look at our plans. Everything is ready. Our revolutionary apparatus will go off tomorrow morning."

I try: "Did you transfer certain projects from Venice to Milan? Vice-presidential kidnapings?"

But he never answers my questions. At least not directly. In turn he asks me, firmly, "Do you come from Brusò?"

"How did you know?"

No reply. I try again: "I find the idea of vice-presidential kidnapings fascinating and uplifting, especially on account of its ironical implications. Perla Manzoni's interview with one of the leaders was carried by *Milano Sabato* and also by avant-garde religious magazines in Scandinavia and in Holland. She said the young man had no beard or anything. In other words, he looked perfectly integrated. Is that sort of a camouflage?"

He looks at me without expressing anything. He questions: "When you went to Brusò to look for Spada, was Josiah Benn's son there too?"

"Not even Spada himself was there; both his daughter and Diana confirmed to me that he's gone to Switzerland; so I was told also by Fornasier's boy. Instinctively I'm alarmed and worried, considering that Spada has the innocence of genius. He ignores the fact that we are all under police surveillance."

"Perla Manzoni's information is irrelevant. The only people who do any sound thinking these days are some priests. The methods are patterned in part on those of our classical anarchists, only without violence, without any assassinations of kings also because"—he smiles somewhat lugubriously— "there aren't any kings. And as far as we are concerned, tell me, has there ever been a time in our history when we haven't been under police surveillance of one kind or another? Here is Daphne."

I had recognized Daphne immediately by myself, not because I had ever seen her before but because of Ferro's succulent descriptions. As she advanced toward us I recognized her better and better, and my mouth watered. Quite mature, which makes her the right thing for me at this point, because a woman like that stimulates my present need to undertake sinful acts in full lucidity and awareness.

By way of opening she spoke to me about Rodolfo Spada with a mixture of possessiveness and contempt which suited me perfectly because it immediately gave me a strong desire to crush her, demolish her. I told her I had gone to look for the master at Brusò, but he was no longer there. Fled to Switzerland, probably.

Daphne in a throaty, lazy, comfortable voice: "No, no, I'm ready to swear to you that he's still there in Angelantonio's house. I know Rudy Spada well and I'm telling you *he has touched bottom.* He has abandoned the struggle and there he is, like the silkworm, in a cocoon. But some day he too will be reached by *pollution* of *all* waters and he'll be submerged *like everybody else* in fetid, poisonous waters."

She gave me a long talk on ecological subjects; she imagines Venice eventually sunk in mud and inhabited by fat excrement-eating snakes, mammoth rats, carnivorous plants. Now really. I am Diego Boldrin. I am the proud grandson of Diego Boldrin, highly esteemed official of the Magistrato alle Acque, the body of experts who have kept watch over our lagoon waters since the glorious days of the Venetian Republic. So whatever she said, I contradicted Daphne point by point. Besides, excellent technicians have gathered here from all over the world, and we are all filled now with hope and vitality. Warming up, both Daphne and I started using arbitrary arguments and false data—mine vital, hers macabre—but it was she who started fabricating them. I said, looking greedily at her, "Damn you all, you want decadent death in Venice, but we'll make it tough for you!"

Finally we turned away from ecological themes and toward evening she made me sense, in a flash, that she was available for love. Love with me. I'm sure it was one phrase of mine that vanquished her: "If we must treat each other roughly, let's do it in the proper place." Then we began to laugh.

After making love, we started laughing again, speaking English—which I noticed I speak quite well—joking on the different meanings of the word *pollution,* like adolescents. The kind of life I lead, moving around all the time on assignments, forces me to prolonged periods of abstinence; hence, when things go well I perform prodigalities, I provide furious love, of supreme quality, prime marrow stuff all of it. During peak moments I was afraid the whole city would hear me roar like a wild Venetian beast, my authoritative incitements, and her raucous, ecstatic, profoundly convinced groans. After the job was done, she offered me Benedictine and brandy, and I drank the mixture as if it had been beer.

I left Daphne buried in sleep. With renovated strength, as in flight, I went back to the garden. Here I found Camentini with two people sitting at his table, Ferro and his girl, a blonde, very young and sturdy.

He introduces me to her as "poet Boldrin" and introduces

her to me: "Ginetta Spadone." Hearty handshake between this blooming Ginetta and myself.

I say, "I see you're all together, so I suppose that you, Ferro, and you, Camentini, know each other."

"Don't ever forget that I am not Ferro at the moment, I am an American producer, Perlmutter." The Spadone girl laughs in a beautiful rustic tone. "Where are your pals, Molisani and Brunetti?" Ferro-Perlmutter asks me. I'm sure I don't know. "Then I'll tell you: Brunetti is back at his university, which is open for the moment, and Molisani is at the hunting lodge where young Benn and some others have gone too. At the Spadone villa there were only four of us" —he sparkles with pride—"when they came to search it."

He wins: I am stoned with surprise. It's as if an obsessive fantasy came palpably true. "To search it? Agents?"

"Two of them. Men with rather primitive minds."

Curiously, however, my electric charge is mounting, I am dripping with energy and avid curiosity. "But the master wasn't there, was he? Isn't he in Switzerland?"

"No. Actually, the evening you came there with those two other fellows, he was there but he didn't show himself, though observing you with paternal affection from a window. When the investigators came he happened to be at the hunting lodge." He explains to Camentini: "Spada is an absolute genius. A basic master. The idea of individual salvage of the mind. The idea of a tomorrow, of a suddenly revealing dawn. The ever renewed expectation of the significant event thrown into time, into life, like a seed, a sparkle of the imagination, which catches and becomes living reality."

Camentini, gloomily: "You like those ideas, Ferro, because you're always ready to stage a happening, but this happening of yours may very well turn out to be your going to jail. You said Benn's son is still there?"

Again the Spadone girl bursts into spectacular rustic laughter: "When they came to search the house, Benn was somewhere around the countryside with Margherita, there were only the four of us in the house."

Ferro's talk. "It was one of the fullest and most satisfactory experiences in my life. My nerves held beautifully. More than that, everything seemed to move according to my stage directions, which I improvised as we went along. Don't interrupt me, Boldrin, I agree with you completely: it wasn't fiction, it was reality, I know, all of us are suspects, on police files. But it so happens that the agents who came to search the old Spadone villa at Brusò had apparently been invented by your comic playwright, Goldoni, so they were ready to fall into the simplest farcical traps. They were confronted by the four of us, two couples: this young lady who is here with me, and Genzianella with the Fornasier boy. Don't interrupt me, Boldrin. Vittorino is neither demented nor retarded: he's been instructed by Spada and has taken his exams, not at the Brusò school, which is lousy, but at the Caerne one, which is good, and he has passed.

"The only drug which those simple men could have heard of must have been cocaine, as in the twenties. I placed an eighteenth-century snuff box on my desk, filled with a nice snowy powder, a mixture of flour, salt, sugar. They confiscated it for further inspection. They also took away plants gathered by other friends on the Aegean seashores. Describing these colorful beauties, I dropped more than once into my talk the adjective *psychedelic,* of which they made a note. They confiscated two guns and a few knives. And manuscripts, including a mimeographed copy of my masterpiece, *The Padua Dead,* and my first treatment for a script on kidnapings of vice-people, an idea which I consider one of the wittiest of the moment. I am ready to accept the hypothesis that the police had been sent to us upon solicitation from the Group, represented in this case by Josiah C. Benn. And I have no doubt that at the bottom of all this there is also the unmistakable hand of your beloved chief, Benito Giuseppe Crocetti Vidal. It is quite evident that rather than help me in my legal difficulties, the accursed virgin has acted as an informer to Benn senior.

"The supreme moment came when the investigators asked me about myself. I can see it in your eyes, Boldrin, how you envy me that exhilarating moment when they asked me, 'Does Remigio Ferro live here? The records indicate that he lives here with Rodolfo Spada.' Immediately and convincingly I became the producer, Perlmutter. 'Whose records?' I shook my head as if to dismiss an irrelevant subject. I realized, however, that it was biologically impossible for me to imply that Remigio Ferro was a negligible person, so I said that of course I knew of him but that no one had ever seen him around there."

I abandoned Ferro as he was having this attack of self-admiration; suddenly my mind went back to Spada and I measured the whole extent of my dereliction and culpability. Not erotic impulse but an obscure strategic instinct led me to Daphne. She was wide awake, sitting in front of the mirror, and she welcomed my reflected image with a smile. I felt that she, somehow, was to blame; standing like that behind her back, I could easily have strangled her.

She stopped me, addressing my image in the mirror: "Diego, if you ever listened to people, you would have registered a proposal I made to you, to have the Dean receive you in his office, so you could discuss everything with him, including your own position in the Organigram."

The Dean meant Benn, Josiah C. It's like a nickname now

but it is also an allusion to his academic past, of which he is proud. I immediately saw myself in the position of the young and bold gangster apprentice who has not yet sunk in mud up to his neck but who has been favorably mentioned in the high echelons of the gang; hence he is admitted very secretly to the presence of the supreme chief, the one of whom the other young criminal operators are never told the whereabouts or even the name.

Dean Benn's vital statistics and his speech. Significant man of our time. At the center of a vast power system, he uses it as a neutral machine, varying its contents according to the interests of the moment. In other words, as with the typical man of power, there is no rapport between him and the truth in regard to facts, ideas or feelings. The absence of such a rapport in B. G. Crocetti Vidal is, I believe, less pernicious because it is covered with words and phrases which are always totally deprived of any practicable meaning. Dean Benn, though not as young as B.G.C.V., is similar to him in appearance—affable, well fed, same type of glasses, etc.—but the moment he opens his mouth, the impression he makes is quite different. He speaks Italian, the language of his mother, like an old gentleman with homespun, stupid mannerisms, even when he expresses ideas and intentions that are most likely to ruin one of his fellow men. He is perfectly capable of using an expression like "Hoity-toity!" with a little smile of conceit. I notice and enjoy these details because I am a philologist.

Of German birth and education, Benn arrived in America not as a persecuted exile but comfortably after the war like some of the space scientists. I have visions of him invading America aboard a gigantic Volkswagen. His father, a church administrator, gave him at the start an easily Americanizable

Christian name because he thought that America was the most religious country in the world.

Before giving me his long talk, the Dean walked around his large Renaissance desk to receive me in the middle of the room; we are in the Orsenigo degli Specchi palace, on whose main floor the Group has installed its sumptuous offices, complete with archives, electronic machinery and everything. The man held my hand softly in both his own for a long while, made me sit on a tall chair, equally Renaissance, and went back to settle himself again in his own chair behind his desk. He never even hinted at the fact that my visit had been arranged by Daphne, while I still bore the marks of her unbridled love on my face. Then he began:

"Deep down in my soul there wasn't any doubt that you would be a correct young gentleman, but, goodness me, seeing you in person beats my rosiest expectations. I look at your clothes, your haircut, your manners, and God be praised, I see nothing, absolutely nothing of the pagan deviltries that are the vogue nowadays. Let me tell you in perfect confidence: one could have been justified in nurturing some suspicion, uh uh, had one judged you only on the basis of reports brought in by some of the most acute and trustworthy Group investigators. Well, no, the impression I have is excellent. I wish my son were like that; I find his behavior quite disgusting. You see that I speak to you as to a friend. Everything looked fine, the boy seemed to have found his way, and now, instead, he ends up in a veritable full-fledged den for little knaves and harlots, complete with madam in the person of a female called Spadone, and, to round out the picture, with a sprinkling of those irreligious, or, God forbid, pseudo-Christian intellectuals whom I call agents of the ideological conspiracy whose purpose is the indoctrination of the young. And now that I see you, Boldrin, I can't fathom why on earth you should have gone to that ill-famed den, further-more accompanied by two of those bearded vagabonds who are now plaguing even the most civilized places in Europe and America. Licentiousness, Boldrin, treacherous permis-siveness. And mind you, I don't mince my words, I include also individuals connected with our Group. I am not refer-ring to the notorious Rodolfo Spada, who was brought into the firm by heaven knows what subversive forces and was sent packing in the very first hours after we took over. I'm referring to people who are associated with the Group; you might say that they don't occupy really vital positions, but I'll tell you they can be even more damaging that way—subterranean infiltrations, I know you grasp my meaning exactly. But at this point, heaven be praised, power, with the responsibilities deriving from it, is represented by your hum-ble servant whose policy is crystal-clear; I don't mind telling you that what we need in the Italian structures of the Group is a nice healthy investigation, and if necessary, a good purge. In spite of his merits, my friend Crocetti Vidal is somewhat in the clouds, especially when he confronts me with what he calls ground-breaking ideas or provocative thinking; he is an engaging speaker and a very efficient organizer, but there are little things which escape him, or which he doesn't call by their right names, whereas I call a spade a spade. And then, he doesn't always exercise due cautiousness in delegating power, or he allows adventurers to become Group stockhold-ers—I am referring to a certain Fornasier—and in the mean-time, Benito Giuseppe shows a total lack of interest in the economic and financial aspects of our enterprises. I've always been suspicious about his refusal to acquire the blue-chip stock of the Group; he suggests religious motivations for his reluctance, whereas to me it smacks of something quite dif-ferent, as I'm sure you understand. At any rate, no such reluctance seems to be felt by his cousin, Elio Vidal, a questionable individual if there ever was one. As you see, I don't spare anybody. Our friend Peritti and our friend Occhietto have freshly arrived from an investigational visit to the Ionian complex, and their report is disconcerting; I must hand it to Peritti that he's always been against that project. Well, better late than never for operating the brakes, or, if necessary, the ax. I know, Boldrin, that you too have paid a visit to the Ionian complex and have briefly indulged in some of its pagan programs. I've heard of a dip in the sea in an extremely scanty costume. I see I'm surprising you. I know all of your movements, dear Boldrin; a responsible executive is informed about everything, for the common good."

(As if evoked by magic, Josiah's two spies, Dr. Peritti and Dr. Occhietto, come in and place themselves at either side of the Dean, respectfully standing there. They don't open their mouths except occasionally to punctuate his talk with one word: "Exactly." Occhietto is very young and sure of himself; Peritti is the oldest and follows Occhietto with admiring affection while the latter is displaying to Benn the fruits of their investigations in the shape of typewritten sheets, microfilms, magnetic tapes, as a traveling salesman would do with his varied and proud sample case.)

"After the Ionian visit, Boldrin, you went to see ambassador Piglioli-Spada, a man, as Occhietto informs me, of a totally different mold from his brother, but definitely senile and useless for information purposes. And from there, my respected friend, you marched straight into the wolf's mouth, to that den for psychotics who are camping on Fornasier's property. Fornasier himself, as we have known for quite a while, is a notorious adventurer and sex maniac, and so is that other individual who is a guest at Brusò, Ferro, the film maker, who, incidentally, goes around under a false name.

Permissiveness and pornography are spreading. After obtaining search warrants we'll make arrests, if necessary. To Occhietto this amounts to a point of honor, and local authorities have shown him extreme courtesy. Let us frankly admit that this feeling of brotherhood among investigative organs is one of the few positive signs in our confused times. Besides, the Group has been promoting and conducting research at the global level on the infiltrations of illegality, disorder, pornography—on all of the present alarming waves of intellectual and moral subversion. When we organize mass exchanges of young people we want them to be sane and trustworthy. I have always been irritated beyond words by the vain, vapid talk of international intellectuals infesting and infecting the area of secular culture; and now there is even more than that, and alarm is added to irritation as we see only too clearly the ever multiplying attempts to bring about an incestuous wedding between Christianity and subversion.

"Boldrin, I'm opening my heart to you; you have good roots, you are redeemable; help us, then, bring up into the light the subterranean infiltrations of evil. We must have the strength to investigate and denounce corrupt consciences one by one. That is our first, luminous duty. That's where the reordering of our priorities must begin. Fight against inner pollution. Ecology of the souls before lagoon ecology! Deep down in the soul, that's where the real polluting action is! A most dangerous action because it is the hardest to identify and to hit. By comparison, it takes nothing to identify and hit—with an ax, if necessary—the moves of common criminals, of militant subversives, of kidnapers. They wanted to kidnap the Vice-President while here on a visit. Holy mackerel! And besides, please note, the visit has been postponed indefinitely."

The pigeons. Very upset but in high spirits I went and found my friends in the garden, including Daphne. Only Ferro was curious to find out what Benn was like. He drank my words:

"Each situation reproduces in small format the general political situations. I saw at work the extrahuman pseudo-thinking central switchboard of an abstract system in which the executive secretary-general himself, B. G. Crocetti Vidal, is perhaps a hardly conscious wheel. I'm sure the peak in psychotechnical perfection in the area is achieved by Dr. Occhietto, who registers everything and everybody on tape and microfilm, and also keeps series of photographs obtained by means of telephoto lenses and special beams, showing for instance the activities in the master's house at Brusò. Through verbal manipulations and audio-visual film cutting you can obtain any results you want; for example, you get the image of Brusò as a den for drug addicts and a center for the instruction of subversives and young prostitutes. I'm sure the reason why Molisani couldn't find a room at the inn and had to spend nights in a sleeping bag is that all rooms were occupied by Occhietto's agents; my instinct suggests that that man will bury everybody else in the Group. Perhaps we have reached a point when comparing someone like Crocetti Vidal to someone like Occhietto would be like comparing an old-fashioned telephone to communication via satellite, or the Quadrilateral to the Pentagon. And by the way, they know all about the 'vice squads' and couldn't care less. At any rate, that Vice-President's visit has been canceled."

Camentini cuts in with dark sarcasm: "That Vice-President was deluding himself if he thought that anybody was seriously interested in kidnaping him. In the Euro-African world, which is the world that interests us most, you may safely say that nobody has ever heard of him. Kidnaping him would mean catapulting him to undeservedly high visibility also in terms of European mass media. Why make him this present?"

Ferro intervenes: "In my script, where you get the real truth, which means poetic truth, the Vice-President's visit does take place. And to protect himself from kidnapings, he always remains aboard his military plane, continuously moving from place to place. He does everything in flight; bathing, putting on his necktie in front of the mirror, talking with European Vice-Presidents, with the cardinal vicar, et cetera."

But I am disappointed. Ferro's scripts don't fulfill me. I need action. I take Daphne away, first we go to her hotel apartment, and there, after the usual B & B, I realize I am caught by a curious and not easily decipherable feeling toward Crocetti Vidal. Impulsively, I put in a call to him.

I've told him things of this kind: "Superchief Benn describes me as redeemable and suggested to me that I take up espionage. Of a new type—soul espionage. Identifying and denouncing the seeds of revolt, of moral opposition to the Group. You will easily understand that after this proposal I feel even less qualified to get into the Organigram. Never had I seen so clearly the danger in those verbal weapons, in those lethal abstractions. Lethal to you too, Benito Giuseppe. In fact, even more so to you than to a person who is basically not structurable, a born outsider to the Organigram, like myself, or like the master, Rodolfo Spada . . ."

His automatic reaction to that name: "Boldrin, you are more or less explicitly suggesting, and not for the first time, that I take remedial action in regard to Spada within our Organigram. But are you in a position to outline a reappraisal and reactivation program? In the past I have articulated certain hypotheses for Spada's possible reinstatement. But this option has lost all credibility, since in the meantime a qualitatively different situation has arisen which would lead us to examine the position of our friend Spada not within the relatively limited area of our organizational structures as within the wider one of civilized society in general. However, I know from Professor Apicetta that due forms of protection for Spada are being studied, both in the legal and in the clinical sense. For that matter, in this particular case the two aspects are, at the relevant levels, coincidental."

I hung up. That is the main trait of our historical period: absolute and definitive impossibility to communicate, in any area, ever. I fell back on Daphne. Just to have something to do in the next few hours, I peremptorily challenged her to give cogent and controllable proof of her ecological love for Venice. I had borrowed Camentini's motorboat. It contains hidden weapons, from the prehistoric sling to the air gun. In the night, in small courtyards with a marble well in the middle, in deserted *calli* and across narrow little bridges, and then also on Renaissance roofs and cornices and on Gothic balconies, everywhere we roused the maleficent pigeons until the city in its most intimate and secret parts resounded with the frenetic cooing of those terrorized parasites.

Upsetting news. We came back to the hotel in full daylight. I was planning to go to Brusò. But instead, we found three people in the living room, two of them from Brusò. One of these, Genzianella, the master's daughter, was snoring on the sofa. The other young lady, Diana, was also asleep, her face hidden in her crossed arms lying on the coffee table. The third person was Remigio Ferro. Perhaps asleep too, but with eyes wide open staring into empty space.

It took them considerable time to wake up and then they looked at us in silence for a long while, as though waiting for our comment on the situation. Genzianella offered us a first hint: "It seems he's here in the Venice jail but they don't tell us anything and they don't let us visit him."

Ferro closes his eyes, waking up; it is never clear whether he is reporting events first-hand or whether he has already transferred them into a script: "Of course he's in Venice; they brought him here in an armored motorboat."

"They brought whom?" I ask superfluously.

Genzianella says, "Papa." Then in a clarion voice: "Rodolfo Spada. My father."

Meanwhile Daphne has ordered *caffelatte*. We drink a lot of it from shiny blue cups with golden edges, and we eat bread, butter, strawberry jam, honey, with the sun sparkling on all this. The tale of the capture and imprisonment of Rodolfo Spada is told in an air of morning festivity by these two beautiful young ladies freshly reinvigorated by sleep, and by Ferro, who adds legendary touches to the story as it goes along.

Rodolfo Spada was *alone* in the villa when a second search was made. After the first one he had advised everybody to pull back to the strongly protected hunting lodge. Now numerous other people had joined the initial group, from different sections of Italy and of Europe, and also people of African and Asiatic origin; they had been put up at the lodge or distributed around the countryside and the surrounding marshes, in ancient peasants' or fishermen's houses; young Benn and Margherita Spadone practically lived in a hunting *botte,* very much in love with each other. Young Benn would say, "If good old Mr. Benn arrives with the cops, before he finds us he'll get stuck in the mud."

Meanwhile, for at least forty-eight hours, continuous phone calls came to the lodge like ominous signals—from Camillo Piglioli-Spada, from Professor Dalle Noci, from

174

Laura and Matilde, finally from B. G. Crocetti Vidal himself and other agents of the Group. Such signals could definitely be interpreted as attempts to recapture the master now escaped, liberated, *evaded into reality.*

Someone from the Group, in fact the celebrated Dr. Plinio, called four times and finally with increasing bitterness he threatened to come in person—all of his postal, telegraphic and telephonic efforts having proved vain—in order to force Spada to fill out and sign several forms with data that the Group demanded of all of its "personnel presently in dead files, formerly in nonorganic subexecutive positions." He also demanded a list of all payments received from any source from the year 1900 on "in order to nullify any possible financial request up to the year 2070 included." Messages indicated that Crocetti Vidal himself intended to come to Brusò.

Generally it was the Fornasier boy who attended to the telephone; his answers, given in the vernacular, were ever more complicated and imaginative. It seems that this malignant epidemic of phone calls was the reason why the master felt momentarily forced to give up his normal contemplative serenity: "Quite evidently now, in their confusion and unhappiness they won't stop at anything, they will use any means in order to try and spread the poisons of unreality among us."

Many of the messages, especially those coming from Matilde Apicetta and Professor Dalle Noci, darkly hinted at the fact that Spada was running serious dangers. The idea was that he should remain quietly at home and gratefully welcome those who only wanted to help him, cure him, save him. Then Spada declared, "Through relatively neutral people like good Matilde or like Dalle Noci, who for the occasion no longer consents to masquerade as an ear-and-throat specialist, the exponents of unreality let me know that I am in danger. It's an extreme attempt to provoke me by challenging my well-known physical and moral courage."

"It was evening," Ferro says. "And it was as though he had foreseen everything. He left all the others either at the lodge or in houses scattered all over the surrounding land and water. He went to the Spadone villa alone. He had a gun with him. At the villa he slept beautifully all night, though missing Diana considerably, and at dawn Venanzio Spadolin (a son of Achille and, it seems, of Countess Spadone) came to warns him that two new agents, brighter than their predecessors, had come to the village for a new search. The two brighties were still at the inn but would arrive presently. Spada gave Venanzio his instructions. Venanzio, twice as big as his father and slightly dumb, understood nevertheless. Spada went downstairs to wait in front of the open house door, gun in hand. When the two visitors were about sixty yards away, Spada aimed the gun at them. Just one instant. Fragment of a second. Venanzio, hidden behind bushes, following instructions, triggered the clay-pigeon machine. A clay pigeon shot off in vibrant flight toward the sky. Spada, calm and precise, took aim, followed the flight with the point of his gun as if drawing a line on the sky with a pencil, scored a bull's-eye.

"The two men approached him. He moved toward them, offered his gun to the first of the two: 'Here. Now you try.' The first man took the gun while the other took advantage of Spada's extended hands to clamp a pair of handcuffs on his wrists. And now they were forced to take him away, to complete an act which was shameful to them and a triumph for him. I could swear it to you, Boldrin, Spada did this for me too, he wanted to offer me this marvelous scene. I understand him in depth, we are brothers. Realizing such a scene together with him would be like the culminating union between his genius and my humble artisanship. Without harming anyone, he has vanquished the unreal ones. Somewhat, if you wish, like the officer in *The Grand Illusion;* by attracting the fire on himself he has allowed all of his dear companions, less strong than he, to remain in safety, each with his own head, in reality. Peasants and fishermen took their caps off as he passed by, handcuffed. Women threw flowers. I should have been at his side! But I too will challenge the unreal beings, unequivocally! I demand my prison term!"

Diana, Genzianella, Daphne went on drinking their *caffelatte* along with Ferro's words, visibly feeding on them. There they were—three women whose very different lives have been brought into focus, invented almost, by Rodolfo Spada . . .

Legal Proceedings. Then toward evening Laura and Matilde Apicetta arrived. Their weapon is a rough-and-ready practicality. They thank Diana *for having been close to poor Rodolfo and having been good to him.* Diana smiles and doesn't even bother to answer. The ladies give assurance that they have already provided legal protection. First-rate lawyers, the best in Venice, Fontana and Fassola.

I attack the two ladies at once: "You are not at the center of reality, of problems. The Group is trying to ruin Spada because he supports the idea of the sudden light of dawn and of mental salvage and fights against the idea of equalized priorities known also as homogenized options. Spada's subversion, of which he himself is not aware, since it's as natural to him as breathing, consists of opposing a world where all heads have the same spherical shape and are all lined up in a row, giving the appearance of abstract forms and yet capable of harboring the most criminal plans. Don't ever forget, dear ladies, that we massively reject the idea that the master may be mentally ill."

"Boldrin dear, as usual I don't understand you well but I'm so glad to see you again. However, believe me, you do have rather a tendency to make a mess of things." While saying this, Laura Spada looks at me with a kind of icy tenderness, of razor-sharp warmth, of masterful submissiveness which, I know, will make me feel dizzy.

But Matilde Apicetta cuts in with some unexpected theories of hers: "Boldrin, you must keep in mind that the executive inspector, Josiah C. Benn, is a very sick man who hasn't had the courage to follow his own premises; sexual experimentation at the Ionian center was an idea *he* brought from America. Now all work at the center has stopped. Elio Vidal's father is dead, that wonderful, pink old man. Besides, Benn is suffering from serious rheumatism and arthritis. I have warmly urged him to go to Babiana Terme for mud therapy and then go to the right clinic for a long period of rest. He is a very confused man. Now he has become a great patriot, has developed sexophobia and is active in the law-and-order movement. He loved his Italian mother, but copulation with her would have been unthinkable, so he took refuge in his Italian wife, who turned out to be unfaithful. Now he seems to be seeking fulfillment in love of country.

"What the Group calls the reordering, or also, the redimensioning of priorities means among other things that Benn and the whole Group from now on will want to have little or nothing to do with us. I mean us disorganized Italians, impulsive and flighty. As for poor Rodolfo, you may say whatever you please about his mental health because you speak as an adoring disciple and I actually admire you for that. In practice, however, not to admit Rodolfo's insanity at the legal level would be double insanity. For that matter, dismissal of the case and release from prison seem like logical options. Actually, no one ever examines these situations in depth, so everything in the end depends on formalities, as for example the fact that those drugs apparently were not drugs, that having had Ferro as a guest doesn't constitute conspiracy in crime, and that Rodolfo holds a regular permit for the gun, which, incidentally, he used to shoot a clay pigeon, so he could just have been practicing in view of the opening of the hunting season." At this point, in her calm didactic tone which is like a hallucination to me, Matilde Apicetta concludes, switching to the familiar form of address: "Don't you worry, Diego; we'll take care of the dear sick man."

"Poor mad Rudy, he just fired a shot in the air, though," Daphne says to infuriate me, thus securing for herself the ecstasy of the massacre which I shall perform on her.

"If he had wanted to shoot a man down, he would have done it perfectly, even from a great distance," Laura says soberly, but with pride.

XXII

"Since those two boys have disappeared too, the whole house has become a little bit like the chapel; a feeling of abandonment, of spoliation, has spread all over it. Bice and Flora are getting more senile by the minute. You, Adele, seem particularly saddened by the absence of those two young men. You go to bed even earlier than you used to, and as you can see, I follow you closely. But nearly all young people nowadays are like that. All over Italy, all over Europe, there are these herds of young people aimlessly wandering here and there, uttering a monosyllabic sound every once in a while, a mewing, a neigh, to indicate that they need food. They don't need much, since they are often drugged.

"The *prefetto* of the province called me, showing extreme courtesy, but it makes no difference now. Nothing makes any difference. Not to mention those phone talks with Crocetti Vidal. I can't clearly figure out who he is. Who is he? And who is that other telephonic nuisance, Signor Peritti? And what is 'the group'? All questions that are left dangling in the air. They must all be people set in motion by Maria Laura to try and reach my brother, or more exactly, her husband, and have him, one hopes, locked up. Perhaps this 'group' is a detective agency. But what need was there for it? Maria

Laura knows perfectly well where her husband is; all she has to do is send up that doctor, Dalle Noci, with a couple of male nurses, to pack him off. Or Maria Laura herself . . . She is small but she is very tough; she could do the whole job herself. Maria Laura . . .

"I feel I've reached closing time, the hour of reckoning. I can't explain it any better, Adele, I feel an urge to tell everything that goes on within me, or that has been going on through the years. For instance, I feel I must tell you that I have been attracted to Maria Laura. There have been occasions, not too frequent but not too rare either, when I have discovered that I desired her. The presence of vice in her, something about her eyes, something ignoble. The great ladies, the Guermantes, the Hapsburgs, have always communicated very little to my senses. Genzianella has inherited from her mother that touch of the vicious little monster which is concealed behind her clean, outdoors aspect. My brother became fascinated with Maria Laura as he saw her ride on horseback, whereas I'll admit that what attracted me, if anything, was something a little filthy that I saw in her. But you sleep and don't listen to me, Adele; it's better that way . . .

"I must have fallen asleep too. I have the impression it's already dawn. And it is rather cold. No breeze; a still coldness. I felt it as it began last night. I told you, Adele, about this feeling of abandonment, as if the iciness from the chapel had spread to the whole house, to the whole . . . Adele? Adele?"

XXIII

Rodolfo Spada:

Vittorino Fornasier passed his exams as an outside student after having been prepared by me and having been completely cured and immunized, especially by my daughter, who gave him massive doses of reality and of psychosomatic affection. He gave random answers to his examiners, mainly using his imagination, and passed with flying colors. Then one day, shortly after my return from jail, the schoolmaster from Caerne turned up here.

The Caerne schoolmaster is a middle-aged man bearing evident marks of a life never disturbed by the search for success, and much dedicated to significant dialogue with himself. He has a French, or perhaps Chinese mustache, and a relentless precision in his look. When he came here, the first person who saw him was Margherita Spadone, who, besides protecting my liberty, is even more keen on protecting that of young Benn, whose child she is expecting.

The schoolmaster, who knows everybody, asked Margherita about the other twin, and about Vittorino, and Luigi.

"My sister is in Venice with Perlmutter, the producer; Luigi is on the phone talking with friends in Texas; and Vittorino, I don't know, he lives somewhere up in the trees."

In contrast to the normally annoyed behavior of importunate visitors when they receive answers of that sort, the Caerne schoolmaster immediately started to laugh. He said that he actually wanted to see me. But in case I didn't want to see him, he would perform an about-face and go back home on his motorcycle.

So, in a jolly mood, Margherita brought the man to me, not here at the villa where I am now, but at the hunting lodge where I was then; he sat down, and for a long while we stared at each other without uttering a single word.

Diana is still in Switzerland with my daughter, Ferro and the other Spadone twin; they have followed my instructions to escape there in case something ominous happened to me; from Venice they went to Lugano, after having a basket of food and a few tablets of Valium delivered to me in jail. All things considered, Ferro's troubles are more serious than mine, except that those two Venice lawyers have now taken a liking to him for his activities as film maker accused of abstract crimes; and Ferro may get out of it by being abstractly sentenced to a jail term of a few months which he won't have to serve, thus avoiding the discomfiture of a prison such as I had to endure.

During that first visit from the Caerne schoolmaster, after he had been sitting in front of me for some time, our prolonged silence was interrupted by the telephone; it was Diana from Lugano.

She tells me things like: "Don't feel too confident. They let you out of jail, but you never can tell. Come here, it's the land of Risorgimento exiles; you remember our talks, right on the first day?"

Her voice carries along with it a vision of her happy eyes and of everything; I am entirely permeated with felicity. I tell her, "You are speaking of legendary times. Then love and adventure easily mingled with historical action. Would you like me to read to you some wonderful pages by Nievo?"

"Don't read pages over the telephone, it would cost us a fortune."

Then Ferro comes to the phone: "Permit me to fight your enemies. I demand it. I deserve it."

I tell Ferro, "You don't run any great risks. The worst that can happen is that you get a suspended sentence."

Clearly he doesn't listen to me, but he likes his own line and he repeats it: "Fighting your enemies. I demand it. I deserve it."

As I hang up, I discover that the bright eyes of the Caerne schoolmaster are fixed on me. His Franco-Chinese mustache seems tacked onto his red, substantial, wine drinker's nose.

"You miss Diana and your daughter tremendously," he says. He knows everything.

I ask him how it happens that he knows everything. He settles himself firmly in his chair, moves his hands forward as if to frame his talk within good, solid gestures; "I've been observing you a lot, from a distance, and then when the agents came I saw you being carried away. I would talk about you with my students. If you hadn't received me now I wouldn't have taken offense. There's a good deal of truth in what the countess says, that these boys and girls are orphans. If I hadn't been sure that you would be good for them, I would have come here and smashed your head, the more so since Luigi's father was my friend, but then others too."

He has also been friends with Achille Cedolin, the sailor-astronomer, since the time they were children; the school-master was born right there, in Caerne, and so was Achille. After taking his doctor's degree at Padua the schoolmaster could probably have had what is known as a brilliant academic career. I haven't the slightest doubt. But instead he came back here, to be able to live, as he puts it, within the right proportions. He is so talented, and now he lives here out of sight, having managed to protect himself very successfully against success. Evidently Achille must have told him a little bit about our way of life. And I'm sure Achille had the schoolmaster in mind when he once said, "The best Italians are those who are officially considered failures."

He has asked me, without stupid insistence, to tell him the story of my short imprisonment, so I told him a few things: they came to arrest me, I said, or rather, to be more exact, at first I thought they had come to get me and shut me up in a lunatic asylum, the same that happened to the poet Tasso and to others; but it soon became evident that they were actually making an arrest, possibly as a consequence of the search they had been conducting in the house, or perhaps the final stroke was the shot that I fired, which might have appeared to be aimed at frightening them, as indeed, in my early intentions, it probably was. At any rate, considering their conception of the contemporary world, it could easily be predicted that they would picture our house as a den for drug addicts dedicated to pagan pleasures. What nonsense. Their imaginations are so dried up that they cannot conceive of the existence of human beings who with small financial resources manage to live fully and agreeably, together, yet each one totally individualized and free, et cetera. The Caerne schoolmaster, however, has a keen eye and a great deal of imagination. He saw me being taken away from here and taken to Venice like a galley slave. I confirm to him what he already more or less imagines.

I found the façade of the Venice jail very attractive; I shall not speak of the interior. Without forgetting the general situation and its considerable discomforts, I must say I detected in my jailors a touch of respectful embarrassment. I haven't the slightest doubt. As for discomforts, I tried to set against them the results of my physical and moral education. I had been in jail only once, as a boy during the war period like so many others; I must say that my previous experience proved of no use, as in the meantime it had been completely erased from my memory. The only thing I remembered slightly was the feel of the handcuffs around my wrists. I'd like to say in passing that they seemed less uncomfortable this time, but I may be wrong; the fact is that however disagreeable, they seemed not to have been designed as positive and intentional instruments of torture.

Confined within a very restricted area, I improvised some systematic muscular and respiratory exercises of minimum motion and maximum results for keeping in good shape. Curiously, among the other inmates I found one who recalled many of my articles; I am vain, hence listened to him with delight. This companion, and others less given to reading, often impressed me with the simple direct character of their humanity. They were incomparably more interesting and tridimensional than those human abstractions that plagued the publishing house after the catastrophe perpetrated there by the Group.

At some point they told me that two lawyers had arrived and that I was allowed to speak with them. I would have refused, but curiosity prevailed. Besides, among my unpleasant sensations, the only one that had a chance to be even worse than physical discomfort, was boredom; maybe, I told myself, here was the chance for a short relief from it.

Both these lawyers have surnames starting with an F, but I don't remember them, so to me they are F-F.

Both F's look distinguished, gray-haired and gray-dressed; real class, as they say. From the way they looked at me, especially the taller one with very dark eyes—as mine were before Diana's revelation—you could see a genuine desire to be of help. Behind that solicitous look, however, I detected the presence of a secret background which I proceeded to explore. Even back there, however, I didn't discover any scheming or deceit but rather, as a matter of fact, a kind of apprehensive respectfulness. Pretty dull people, obviously; but not wholly unreal. Or rather, not unreal *per se.* But the fact is, they must have received certain "guidelines," and they automatically followed them in their actions. I was struck with the certainty that this core of automatism and unreality must somehow be connected with the Group; and from that moment on it was impossible for me even to perceive F-F, let alone listen to them.

Now rumor has it that those two lawyers did everything, spurred to action by two women, my wife and Matilde Apicetta, particularly the latter, who in order to have me liberated is supposed to have made use of her old friendship with B. G. Crocetti Vidal. All this I have heard from Angelantonio Fornasier, who is here on a visit, shuttling back and forth between the hunting lodge and Babiana Terme. He and Countess Spadone organized a big celebration for Vittorino; we missed Diana and my daughter so intensely that tears came to our eyes.

Fornasier is steaming with indignation at the Group. In fact, he plans to use those two wonderful lawyers, F-F, to bring a series of suits for damages against the Group. That's his business. I carefully refrained from asking him to explain how the Group is supposed to have had me first put in jail, and then to have had me liberated. Naturally I made it clear to him that whoever may threaten to channel the conversation into this veritable carnival of conflicting unrealities will have to be excluded from my presence with the same courteous rigor with which I have more generally excluded anyone that may come and talk to me about the Group and its components.

The Caerne schoolmaster told me that he is a widower. His wife died at twenty-two. "Do you understand? At that age Death took her as though she had been his property." After an adequate silence he adds, "But the time spent with her was consistently spectacular." Another long silence; then, well settled in his chair, with effective motions of his strong arms: "In the old days, if people here found out that a girl was good at making love she was immediately called a whore. Now everything has changed. Young fellows have other problems, but usually not that one. Who is Boldrin?" He doesn't wait for an answer. "He came to see me, he complained that you don't want to see him. You are right, he must be on his own. He is always in a frenzy; first-rate young man, though."

"Very first-rate."

"Also young Benn's father came to see me, along with two melon-headed fellows wearing glasses and looking exactly like him. One is called Occhietto, the other one I don't remember what." He grunts and seems to doze off. Then suddenly lighting up again: "Spies. Curious thing, from the way Occhietto looked I thought he had come here to *sell* drugs—a sort of traveling salesman in dope—while he turned out to be the opposite; he said, 'We are conducting statistical research, Professor, you know,' but after all, what I then told him could fit both eventualities, whether he was a pusher or a spy; I explained to him that there is not sufficient affluence around here for anyone to introduce the habit of expensive stuff like drugs on a large scale; and besides, of course, you would have to erase millennia of a tradition largely represented by wines and spirits. He looked very depressed. And as a matter of fact, even if he is not a sales-man, he produces the same results in spreading the word about drugs among people. The other two, especially Benn, are very curious about the life of the young people around you, and how they make love."

"The usual voyeuristic curiosity."

"They call it research on the perils of sex. What do *they* want? Group masturbation?" Mentioning local love stories, he gets emotional. Eight months from now the child of young Benn and Margherita Spadone will be born. He whispers, "In a sense the baby will be a grandchild of mine," informing me by implication that between him and the Countess Spa-done there has been what my father would have called a *liaison.* "After my wife died, what could I do? She would come to me, she sang, she found everything *so sweet.* "

Vittorino, Margherita with Benn, Luigi and others gather around him and he says, "Yours is a more difficult revolution than usual because it is bloodless—in fact, invisible and ex-clusive." They smile, amused, and he goes on, "You, like Spada here, are the kind of persons who don't need anybody and therefore are most irritating to all those people who are stuck in boredom and uninventiveness. You run on the prin-ciple that either all moments in life are worthwhile, or none of them are. So you make all of them worthwhile." They don't understand him very well, but they laugh and cheer.

I let him talk because he seems useful and pleasant. I mention my old friend Daphne to him and the recent ecologi-cal direction her social activities have taken; he explains immediately: "All over the world now you see on the one side people denouncing environmental dangers, poisons, suffoca-tion, fumes, and on the other, industries denying everything; and good-bye everybody. All things can only start from the individual mind. Each mind must be educated by its own means. Political, moral, economic, ecological problems must be experienced"—he stares at us with eyes wide open—"*the way you experience art.*"

Then he is back on love: "In a place like this you have the leisure, the abundance of time for the adequate development of love. First the preparatory work, exchange of looks, mutual attentions, then the proper wine and food around you, and festivities; and taking care of each other in sickness. For a long time," he goes on, "for a long time now I have ceased to worry about galaxies. Let's stick to events within the framework of real life, within our own actual proportions. At the present moment it's a good idea to devote much time to living, which to some people would mean doing nothing—an important occupation, feeling your feelings and thinking your thoughts one by one from all possible points of view. Your idea is right, salvaging the mind and operating it fully, but then, there is so much to do even in the most practical, immediate sense. For instance: saving the book."

"Which book?"

"The book as a type of thing, as a usual human object."

He admits all of this will not be easy and he advises me: "Now you pass for an innocuous madman and that wouldn't be so bad, but your supporters' notion is dangerous because they want to take that label away from you and replace it with that of a genius, whereas you must strive for a no-label status, maintain your independence, otherwise you'll be caught in a trap. Of course you may very well be a genius, but you must ignore the fact. You must prevent them from bothering you, wasting your time with searches and arrests. You must show that you are even more unambitious, more obscure, more unfit to play the game—someone they can forget about without any danger, or envy, or remorse. Then, instead of searching your house, they'll start searching each other's houses, and in the end there will be no trace of them left because they will have canceled each other out."

He talks all the time. I let him talk; the boys and girls like him. When I start listening to him again he is saying, "Most government people are, at best, useless." After the news we watch some old American comic pictures on TV. Pies hit faces in an ever quicker and happier tempo. When it's over, a commentator wearing glasses appears on the screen, much resembling Crocetti Vidal, but with long hair. He suggests he is going to "detect a line of development, to see how the structure of the film vehicle permits the inclusion, at the highest and most valid levels, of archetypal patterns of dream . . ." The Caerne schoolmaster recognizes the commentator, exclaiming, "Rosario!"

They turn off the TV and he explains: "Your friend Ferro has a fixation about Rosario. All you have to do is mention Rosario to him, and he goes into a crisis."

"I remember Ferro's story about the Arnaut Daniel lines."

"Rosario and I were schoolmates at Padua. His name is Rosario Trendolini but he is so prominent that Rosario is enough, as with Dante. Once in a long while I go to Rome and then I ask him, 'Rosario, whom are we allowed to mention at the moment? Who is excluded? Kafka? Musil? Feuillet? Verne? Pantaloon?' He doesn't even listen to your questions. He never reads anything. He is always sleepy. How do *you* sleep?"

"I sleep very well."

"I do too."

We exchange a few ideas on evening remorse, and on the good habit of examining one's conscience before falling asleep. In this sense he feels he is doing much better than he used to. I have the same feeling. I told him about my plan to achieve a position as a substitute teacher, when the moment comes.

We were rambling on like that when Diana, Genzianella and Ginetta Spadone came in, bringing a Ferro destroyed by emotion. It was one of the most pleasant moments in my life. We didn't say anything special; I exchanged many kisses with Diana and my daughter, and of course no one mentioned my liberation except Ferro, albeit indirectly. He insists he wants to fight against those whom he calls my enemies. That's his problem. He maintains that Crocetti Vidal, who has reappeared briefly in my thoughts a couple of times but has now totally disappeared again, will soon arrive here. I calmed Ferro down by promising him that if it should happen I'll let him receive Crocetti Vidal and deal with him in any way he wants, provided I don't have to see him. Angelantonio Fornasier joined us for dinner; he confirms the presence of a number of people around here, especially at Babiana Terme, where they go for mud therapy. It seems that not only my wife and Matilde are there, but also Benn senior, and Professor Dalle Noci, the one who gave me those pills; and finally, big surprise, none other than Camillo Piglioli-Spada, my brother.

XXIV

Diego Boldrin:

The situation is absolutely wide open.

Camentini tells me that Ferro is back from Switzerland to claim "his prison term." He feels his nerves would hold beautifully at the happening-trial, which should establish whether those minors have been corrupted by him in real life or in screen fiction. Ferro would like to turn the trial into a tremendous mass-cultural event, with large employment of the media. He is deluding himself. He won't get anywhere, because even if there were a trial, which is unlikely, his new Venice lawyers, Fontana and Fassola, would, after the customary delays and postponements, at the very best be able to get him a nominal sentence for a short prison term which he wouldn't have to serve, anyway.

Fontana and Fassola find Angelantonio Fornasier much more interesting as a client. He is planning very long and elaborate legal proceedings against the Group. "Besides," he has said, "I absolutely intend to expose the violent and subterranean methods by which they have tried to appropriate large slices of our cultural and economic life. As of now," he adds, "I am again making a lot of money. Money has never meant anything to me, so this time I'll spend it to make trouble for the Group." Among other things, he is investing furiously in the art market. "And I hold a large interest in a firm that produces pop-music recordings. It's a magnificent language, which I understand." Meanwhile he is studying law day and night. He is a slow lip reader; books cost him great effort. He is an honest man. In other words, a man of genius. Nowadays honesty must be recognized as genius: a lucid, sharp, instinctive, compassionate view of men and events. I am elaborating on old sayings of Spada's.

I ask Fornasier, "And what about B.G.?"

He answers with a sigh, "Poor Peppino."

A curious reaction. Where is Crocetti Vidal? I'm not asking where he is in reality but in the world where his life unfolds, i.e., in the structure of the Organigram.

One thing is certain: there is open talk going on about New Restructuring. And apparently it has now been confirmed that all projects for new periodicals such as *The Mediterranean Tourist* have been dumped. Two reasons: first, the periodicals already existing, which flourished during the Spada era, have now, through the Restructuring method, achieved their zenith in costs and their nadir in sales; second, the Group, following the advice of electronic computers which give future projections indicating that human familiarity with the written word will reach its terminal stage between April and May of 2017, is transferring almost all of its cultural popularization activities to nonverbal forms of communication.

The latest news is that the Group, without consulting Crocetti Vidal but also without stripping him of his titles, has appointed Dr. Mario Occhietto to a position of high authority. In the New Restructuring, apparently Occhietto is going to bear a traditional but nonetheless glittering title like executive vice-president. He has studied in America and in Sweden, where he received degrees in education and gymnastics; he is described in terms that were once used to describe Crocetti Vidal—an exceptional young man, a born organizer. Part of his training was in the camping industry. To accept the present appointment he apparently put some nonnegotiable conditions to the Group, namely, that the Ionian project be definitely abandoned and that in the newly projected cultural-touristic structures, gymnastics and collective prayer be as obligatory as flag raising. Another Occhietto request is the Group's right to inspect the private correspondence of all employees, whether or not they be part of the Organigram. On the other hand, the terminal date for the period of freeze on all royalties to be paid former contributing writers is moved back from the year 2070 to the year 2017, but then, everybody knows that the extinction of human communication through the written word is predicted at that date, so that the very concept of literary copyright will become irrelevant.

Occhietto, *qua* vice-president, perhaps fancies himself an object of interest to the kidnapers of vice-persons; therefore he goes around always surrounded by a group of very muscular and active young men whose perfectly spherical heads are the size of buttons.

I put in one of my periodical calls to Crocetti Vidal but he doesn't seem to be aware of anything. "Benito Guiseppe," I told him, "here we are, the hour has struck. The Group has come to an inner break, to a decisive split, to a *polarization of the issues.*"

But he, with his usual rotund and liquid voice, explained to me: "My dear Boldrin, ours are creative divergencies which will be perfectly integrated once we extract and articulate their potential positiveness, at the level of dialogue."

Once more I hung up and rushed to Daphne. And I didn't find her.

Restructuring and mourning. I am now at Babiana Terme. Daphne left Venice suddenly and secretly. I had become accustomed to our savage evening encounters; so as I walked around alone in the night through my native city I gasped, I bit the air, and I suppose I talked to myself. In such conditions I was met by the new editor of a Venice daily paper, a Neapolitan who is also a noctambulist; he recognized my wandering shadow and after a very animated talk along deserted alleys he invited me to come back to work at the Venice paper which he now edits; there, in distant years, I had my first job, at sixteen, an infant prodigy.

I told him that perhaps I would accept, provided he gave me carte blanche so I could campaign for a lucid and rational *restructuring* of the chances for intuitive and vital optimism still to be found in spite of all possible disasters and threats; the campaign would have its center in Venetia and its brains in Dorsoduro and Brusò. The editor took me by the arm and affably listened to my long talks, which I immediately forgot. He asked me to allow him time so he could reorganize my ideas in his mind; then he would get in touch with me. We parted at dawn. Shortly after that, studying my face in the mirror I realized that I had suddenly decided to leave for Babiana Terme, where I knew I would find Laura Spada and Matilde Apicetta, hence probably Daphne as well.

But Daphne isn't here. This is what happened: the Ionian center, abandoned by the Group, has been taken over by Elio Vidal personally; Daphne has joined him bringing capital. Matilde explains, with that didactic lucidity which to me is still like a hallucination: "Daphne, if we may put it in these terms, is moving from environmental ecology to internal visceral ecology—ecology within the human body. For a long time it has been conjectured that the most varied illnesses may have their origin in sexual imbalances and insufficiencies. To me, all of this simply means that Daphne's intention is to make clear what the Ionian center is all about; in other words, the clinical-sexual aspects of those structures will be emphasized." Here the lady professor adopts a suddenly flippant tone: "Don't sneer, Boldrin. Do you want to know what *I* think? I think: good, more power to her."

Throttled by memories of my lovemaking with Daphne, I hardly find enough voice to ask, "So you'll go down there on the Ionian Sea?"

"Not I, but probably Laura. For the time being I'll stay on here at Babiana Terme, where I've brought Josiah Benn too; he takes his mud bath every day."

And in fact, Matilde left us a moment later to go and see Benn, who apparently now lives permanently in the mud. So Laura and I were alone. Laura talks a lot, and her voice, however monotonous, makes me dizzy: "Dear Boldrin, I'm so happy to see you again. As you know much better than I, Brusò is only a few miles from here, but we have been advised by Dalle Noci to skip going to see my husband so as to allow him some breathing space, as it were. Dalle Noci is not alarmed, but in a way Rodolfo's insanity, I find, is of the saddest sort—gray, without dramatic explosions. Stagnant. Disappointing. However that may be, it is quite clear, Boldrin, that Rodolfo doesn't want to see either you or me."

Toward evening, walking in the labyrinth-garden with little lamps shining against the dark green foliage, I took her in my arms and said to her, "My dear Laura, I feel this is our last night. The first and the last. We'll wake up in the morning and offer living proof of the sudden-dawn theory, the theory of the revealing tomorrow, when each of us in a flash will see the opening of a new road, and will enter it."

"It isn't the first time that I don't know what you are saying, Boldrin dear, but considering that Rodolfo doesn't want us, and Matilde is with Benn, let's have dinner, you and I, polenta and sausage if it suits you."

Halfway through the dinner I had to get up to take a call from Venice. The editor was coming up with definite proposals. I said to him, "Michelino, I have a lump in my throat. I am strangled by memories of the time when I worked at the paper you now edit. I was sixteen then, serious, active, full of confidence. Brahms' Fourth, Proust, phenomenological criticism—I devoured everything. To write, to persuade, the joy of giving light through the written word, et cetera. Moral peace found in very attentive study. The clear and lively description of a subject, of the state of one's conscience, et cetera. Will I be worthy of myself at sixteen? Let me have one night to think it over."

I went back to the dining table and to polenta and sausage feeling much relieved, recharged. My psychosomatic stock went up. After dinner it took no effort, love just happened without our ever talking about it either before, during or after. She let me do to her anything I wanted. Her perfume is primarily that of soap. Compared to Daphne, it was child's play. For a long while I watched her sleep, reviewing in my mind all that I knew about her life; then I kissed her without waking her up and I fell asleep too; and toward morning *we had the same dream.* We were sailing on a very calm sea resplendent with flaming sunlight, rapidly and in absolute silence; and it wasn't clear who was piloting us. "It's a dream I always have, Boldrin dear, and I assure you the pilot is Rodolfo." At that very moment there was Michelino's call from Venice.

Without preamble he asks me an unexpected question: "Does the name Mario Peritti mean anything to you?"

"An employee of the Group. Rather high in the Organigram. Older than the average. Leaner too. Liver ailment.

Tension. Doesn't particularly get along with B. G. Crocetti Vidal. In the Group's palace in Venice, he and Occhietto were standing on either side of Benn. It was Peritti that brought Occhietto into the Group; Occhietto is the new man and I've heard that Peritti is in love with him."

"He isn't in love with anybody any more because he is dead. He committed suicide in a hotel on the Lido."

I can't find anything to say. I have never had any feelings, one way or another, about Peritti. The Group's inner conflicts, now crowned by no less than a death, have never really touched me, who am organically an alien to the Organigram.

Michelino spoke at length; I listened to him here and there: "The Group people are closing shop here in Venice after having pretended that they wanted to promote Venice as an 'executives' island.' In fact, they are going to leave Italy altogether. I know that Benn is still there at the Babiana mud baths. It has never been clear to me what the Group does, what its point is; maybe you could interview Benn and ask him for us; I heard it has to do with ecology, sexology, also avant-garde Christianity; however, don't write anything too far advanced otherwise I can't publish your article. Our newspaper has a large and stabilized circulation among solid, right-minded people and I want to keep it that way."

"All you've heard about the Group belongs to the distant past. But for that matter, whether the Group upholds a given idea and movement, or the idea and movement exactly opposite, it's all the same."

"Well, see what you can do. I'm happy you're with us again."

Renewed motions of joy and clarification within me. In the meantime, Laura had taken a shower and dressed. She was ready to leave for the Ionian center and then for New York, where, as she said, she is dying to see those wonderful new museums. She took me in her car to the baths building. We exchanged correct kisses and she let me out. I stood watching her go until her car reached the curve. She drives beautifully, not worrying about anything—a taxi driver.

I was curiously fortunate in finding Benn alone. He didn't expect a visit and even less an interviewer; he lies in mud up to his neck so that his head is out in the air and he can breathe and also talk.

That head emerging from mud turns toward me with suspicion. Does he know about Peritti? We don't mention the subject. I smile. I manage the neutral interviewer's tone: "Dean Benn, permit me to ask you an opening question on the Group's cultural activities in Italy. How far are we? And, more generally, my newspaper would be interested in questions of this type: Do you really believe that avant-garde evangelism has any chances in Italy? And what about, within the same framework, art for the masses?" I went along like that for a while, with an assortment of disparate questions.

Interview? Not a chance. He hasn't even heard my words and he speaks in choked, headless sentences: "Absence of all ideals. Spitting in the face of law and order. Contempt toward all sacred values." Then, shifting to a more academic, sermonizing tone: "Here in Italy you missed a splendid chance to associate social demands with the reality of the evangelical word. Now instead you want to associate the evangelical word with subversion. Shame! Good-bye!"

In high spirits, I retort, "You should rather say that your attempt at exploiting fashionable culture and up-to-date science, and perhaps also *chic* religion, blew up in your hands. Periodicals which were excellent now don't interest anybody, and you react to your own failure by proposing to suffocate the human word altogether. Meanwhile Elio Vidal, whose father died amid the roar of bulldozers, is taking over the Ionian center to put its erotic offerings clearly on the market instead of bootlegging them as you were trying to do. Your faithful agent, B. G. Crocetti Vidal, is a flop and so are you all, a total flop, not only biological but also ideological, technological, economic, financial. In all of this, the Group is a model pattern, a perfect example of the typical institutions of our time and of the triad that guides them: abstract and pathological attachment to power; costliness; inefficiency."

For a moment the Dean goes back to the kind of language he used with me in Venice: "You are touched in the head, my dear sir. Goodness me, Boldrin, I thought you were a civil young man but I see you are touched in the head and wicked like all the others."

"Your failure," I proceed quietly, reasonably, "began at the time when Rodolfo Spada, who could have been your main trump, got out of the game, having sensed before anybody else that you had resigned from human life." I conclude with even greater poise: "Spada has defeated you without using violence, indeed probably without even realizing it. You don't realize it either, but Spada is the one who is throwing you out. His escape started the chain reaction. Some morning sooner or later all humane human beings will abandon their respective dehumanizing Groups and perform their individual flights into reality. Please, Dean, observe for instance how many people already are or would like to be at Brusò. You are here in the mud but your son is there. And I very much doubt that at Brusò they will want you, particularly as a grandfather."

The reaction to these very clear and simple words of mine was a wild yell. So I started to yell too, somewhat incoherently, "The battle cry is always the same: I believe in nonabstract people, in the looks and words exchanged between them, in ever-renewed tomorrow-morning, bearer of lucid visions; I even believe in the possibility of new public institutions, healthy and full-blooded, which will dry up the rotten mud and will hold Venice in the palm of their hand, in the sun and in the fog, day and night. You are seekers after death, you have already produced a corpse, now you get out! Out!"

"*You* get out, you accursed creature!" He rises clumsily from his therapeutic slime and grabs a handful of it. He throws it at me. But he doesn't hit me because I shield myself with the door, which I slam behind me as I leave.

Where is our protagonist? I am again in Venice, actually settled here. Every minute I feel like kneeling down to kiss the stones of my city. The master at Brusò doesn't want to see me and I understand him, but I'm sure he would approve of my return here. Everything starts anew; I have my head of today along with the dash of the sixteen-year-old.

In the usual garden Camentini has reported to me that Peritti's suicide has gone practically unnoticed; Occhietto saw to that. Now Occhietto has left, in the company of Peritti's corpse, which will be funereally honored in Rome. No one predicts a resumption of the Group's operations in our country. "But I assure you," Camentini says, "that if they should stage a reappearance, then their machines, their electronic setup, their archives and files, everything will be razed to the ground. There won't be any need to organize complicated kidnaping operations, and the artistic beauties of the Orsenigo degli Specchi palace will remain intact. It isn't a difficult undertaking and I give you my personal and formal guarantee for it." I see him laugh cheerfully for the first time in months.

Although the New Restructuring of the Group will exclude Italy, Dr. Occhietto's authority naturally will not be cut down; he is the perfectly and ubiquitously organigraphed executive, and the omnibus superpatriot, raiser of all flags and defender of all laws and orders. Benn has left too, apparently for a hospital in Spain.

And what about Crocetti Vidal? I called Rome and couldn't reach him anywhere. There are rumors that he too is in a clinic, though here in Italy. In other words, pressing questions have remained unanswered concerning the man who is still to us the leading personage in the Group, the protagonist. Where is Crocetti Vidal? In what conditions? And why?

The situation is wide open.

XXV

It is indispensable, by way of provisional conclusion, to attempt from the inside a further clarification of certain facts and movements.

There is no point in pedantically evaluating the reliability of the Boldrin source. His reports on some events and people provide, in their essential traits, the maximum truth one may ever hope to achieve.

The Group, without admitting it publicly, in fact stating the opposite in their Xerox messages, are abandoning their cultural, publishing, touristic and clinical interests in Italy. Josiah Benn and Mario Occhietto leave our country after the funeral of the late lamented Dr. Peritti, to start elsewhere the complex operations for a New Restructuring on a Global Level. Represented by two of the most eminent Italian lawyers, Fornasier is initiating legal action against the Group which will expand into years or indeed decades. Elio Vidal and Daphne are in the midst of their own restructuring at the Ionian center, where work will be resumed along more decidedly sexological guidelines. Laura Piglioli-Spada joins them and then she will go on with them to New York as a guest of Hugo Crossetti, especially for the purpose of visiting those splendid new museums.

Diego Boldrin walks through Venice not only at night but also at high noon, his head raised and his nostrils open wide, along narrow streets and across small bridges as the warm scent of polenta and fried fish is spreading all over. In his continuous flood of oral reportage, he leaves two principal gaps visibly open, the lot of two people: Camillo Piglioli-Spada and B. G. Crocetti Vidal. Some notes of Rodolfo Spada, which were apparently salvaged by Boldrin himself, contain a passage where those two personages are concisely and curiously compared:

A superficial observer might detect similarities between my brother, himself an abstraction, and B. G. Crocetti Vidal; but actually the two, apart from the fact that my brother is twice B. G.'s age, are very different. I was thinking about that this morning. (Omissis.) The fact is that B. G. Crocetti Vidal, who at a first glance may appear to be made of the same substance and fiber as celery, on the contrary is full of animal juices rapidly circulating in him. His skin, closely observed, always looks a bit greasy; but it's clean grease, as of excellent leather. His main characteristics are intense vitaminization and perfect proteinization. I don't hesitate to formulate the hypothesis that someday he may suddenly come out of the unreality in which he now lives and operates. If that happens, it will be a consequence of my escape. I haven't the slightest doubt.

Boldrin and the others had signaled the presence of Camillo Piglioli-Spada around the Spadone villa at Brusò, but the first person to sight him, all alone, displaced, surprising, was his niece Genzianella. In fact, at first she just sensed his presence. Even before the old ambassador pulled the handle of the old house bell, she opened the door and found herself face to face with him and smiled: "Uncle?" She has told the story herself, and there exists no more reliable source.

Her uncle stares at her with one of his blankest expressions. He doesn't say anything. The girl brings him into the house. She makes him sit down. He is still silent.

She is surprised that he doesn't reproach her for anything —her disappearance from Succaso, the prearranged kidnaping. His look is still blank, yet deep underneath, it seems as though he were holding a secret weapon to be pulled out at the right moment.

In long moments of silence his head falls; several times his chin hits his chest; then she whispers tenderly, "Uncle Camillo, what about a little rest?" But he has dozed off; she listens to his soft snore.

More than an hour has passed. She has gone out on tiptoe, to tell Vittorino. She stays with him for a long while. Suddenly, a raucous call from her uncle: "Genzianella, come here!"

"Yes, Uncle."

"Listen, I saw you, what you were doing with that boy. I always saw you, with the others too, all of them."

"Poor Uncle Camillo, don't tell me you like to watch."

"What do you do, what do you feel with that boy? Or with that sheep, Molisani?"

"They are among the most precious people in my life. When Vittorino was sick I nursed him as if I had been his mother, so to speak."

"Where was his mother?"

"Dead. Extraordinary woman. Chilean and Russian. Angelantonio can't mention her without tears."

There is a long, very heavy silence; then the uncle, heavy, panting: "What do you accuse me of?"

"I don't know, Uncle Camillo."

"So, then you accuse me of something?"

"I don't know, I assure you I don't know."

"You're all monsters. Your mother. That man Vladonicic. You too. They had you meet him, they put the two of you together. What did you do, with Vladonicic?"

"He talked to me in his dialect. He was dying. He kissed my cheeks."

Uncle is again buried in silence. Then he stares directly at his niece; he looks demented rather than lost as he says, "Adele is dead."

"What?"

"Adele, my wife, your aunt, is dead. I was continuously complaining about my own ailments, almost forgetting that the really sick one was Adele. We men are like that, curse us."

His niece is standing still, attentive, considering what to do.

The old man goes on, "I was in bed with her and discovered that she was lying dead next to me."

The girl nods to herself; she goes up to call Rodolfo Spada. Only she could persuade him to see his brother.

When Rodolfo enters the room, Camillo gets up but he goes on as if he didn't perceive the new presence: "I was talking to her, to Adele, I thought she was asleep. Even now I think it was only sleep. I fell asleep myself. The following morning I wake up at dawn, I feel a curious sort of silence around me, full of tension; what can that be? I call her, I shake her, suddenly it's like a revelation, everything becomes intensely clear to me there in the light of dawn, it's as though I remembered something long forgotten. I observe her minutely, I touch her, I realize that she is dead."

Rodolfo, his brother, grabs him by the shoulders with his

iron grip, compels him to sit down, settles him comfortably there: "Now you stay here, Camillo, you stay here with us."

From that seated, tamed posture Camillo seems to recognize him; he raises his eyes toward his brother: "I could have grown fond of you. I always said that to Adele. To Maria Laura too I said that."

"But I believe you, Camillo."

"No! You shouldn't believe me!" He looks scornful, then his eyes become empty, dull. "The truth is I've never been fond of anybody."

His niece asks, "Not even of Amedeo, your son?"

"How can I be fond of him? He is on drugs, curse him."

Rodolfo nods at his daughter: "Let's take him upstairs."

"Come up, Uncle. I'll put you to bed. You stay here with us."

As everybody knows, the principal mode of existence of an individual is his speech. According to information provided by Boldrin, who often called him on the phone, B. G. Crocetti Vidal's speech didn't seem to change during the internal dissensions in the Group. Nor was his decision to go on a trip to Venetia unexpected. Ten days earlier he had made an appointment with Josiah Benn at Babiana Terme to discuss normal restructuring problems; the initial motive for his trip north was only that.

In Rome, he spent a perfectly routine day. In the very first hours of the afternoon he listened in his apartment to a splendid new stereo recording of *Lohengrin.* He left that evening in a sleeping car. Curiously, from Padua, where he got off the train, he drove not to Babiana Terme, but to Brusò. There he didn't manage to talk to Rodolfo Spada (it wasn't clear to anybody, including himself, why he was looking for him), but he was received by Angelantonio Fornasier, who was ready to give him a serious and practical talk which was, however, blocked by the rapid eloquence of Crocetti Vidal, on whose lips some well-known formulas were already prepared; one felt, he said, that there was "basic accord on the relevant issues"; one shouldn't talk of "dichotomies in the true sense of the word"; he rather saw "a structure of radial options, of convergent alternatives."

Then Fornasier managed to tell him, "But you won't find Benn here. He left Italy with Occhietto, shortly after Peritti's funeral."

"I sent a wire to the widow," Crocetti Vidal said in a quiet, affable tone, "and Benn just cannot have left, he has an appointment with me at the Baths' Hotel."

"Let's go there so you can see for yourself. At any rate, you'll find Matilde."

They found her in the living room of her hotel apartment; Remigio Ferro was with her. As soon as he saw Crocetti Vidal enter the room, Remigio whispered words which sounded at first rather mysterious: "Here he is. The curtain rises. My nerves hold excellently well."

He moved slowly toward Crocetti Vidal and stopped in front of him: "You came here to look for your masters and you find a friend instead, that is, you find me. And who was it that sent this friend, me, to receive you? Rodolfo Spada, who had foreseen everything. Spada, the one you despised because he couldn't be structured. So you deprived the firm of a man of genius and you brought in the unreal beings who are now cutting *you* out."

A quick process started at this point, whereby all expression faded out of B. G. Crocetti Vidal's face. His evergreen eyes, now already dull and sparkless, turned to Matilde, who nodded rapidly: "They've left, all of them. But now you are among friends, Peppino, and you know it."

"At the level of dialogue," Crocetti Vidal murmured, but it sounded like a taped voice, built into him.

"That dialogue is closed," Fornasier said, "closed forever, Peppino."

Now all light in Crocetti Vidal's eyes was extinguished; he mumbled monotonously, without listening to himself, "Basic exigencies . . . Developments which involve the whole re-structuring process . . ."

It was at this point that Remigio Ferro grabbed him by the shoulders and shook him violently. The other man produced a vague, weak lament, like that of a dying person justifying his life with words that he neither understood nor heard. "All . . . both cultural and industrial discourse . . . availability of options . . . multiple articulations . . . all . . ."

Now Ferro grabbed his neck. He spoke with furious urgency: "I have understood you, Crocetti Vidal. And now I understand that I have always understood you. It isn't your fault. You don't exist."

Up to that moment Crocetti Vidal had seemed inert, but when Ferro started asking him urgently, "You are a virgin, aren't you? You are a virgin?," then in his eyes a new, unprecedented spark was kindled, later described by Ferro as "a flash of belligerent hatred." Matilde—perhaps coming closer to a truth which can never be reached in the absolute, anyway—would later define it as "a fresh gust of energy, as in a strong adolescent waking up." It was as though certain words never pronounced, certain actions never performed by Peppino when he was a student of supreme capability but all closed within his own industriousness and his cool cleanliness, were now erupting, defrosted; he exposed his ultrawhite teeth in a proud smile; his voice reached the peak of its strength and melodiousness: "Oh, how you would all like to be like me! You degenerates! Putrescent matter! Filth!" Then he sneered threateningly and raised his powerful right leg. It is testified by all those present that he did not seem aware of what he was doing; but the nature and objective of his embryonic motion were clear: kicking Remigio Ferro in the testicles.

There has been much exaggeration on the subject of Ferro's scarce physical energy. And at any rate, no one has ever doubted the quick nervous promptness of his reflexes. He caught Crocetti Vidal's ankle in flight, as it were; and using that (right) leg, again in a manner of speaking, as a handle, all he had to do was give it a little push forward for the other man, balanced on his left leg only, to fall back on the floor. From that moment on, Angelantonio and Matilde, according to their repeated testimony, didn't make a move to separate the two; they followed the developments of the contest as they would a show, or even a ceremony.

Taking advantage of their respective positions, Remigio Ferro was immediately on top of Crocetti Vidal, who was lying on his back; holding him down by the neck with his left hand, he started to slap him systematically in the face with his right hand, palm-stroke, back-stroke, palm-stroke, back-stroke, while staring him in the eye and addressing him in a distinct, rhythmical whisper as if to hypnotize him: "This is the final scene, didn't you know? Well, then, live this moment fully, Benito Giuseppe, the total coincidence between invention and act; live, B. G., live."

Crocetti Vidal, however, had moved his big right knee to the proper position against his adversary's lower abdomen, and so he managed to catapult him backward and liberate himself. He stood up immediately.

For a while the two looked like prizefighters in a ring, dancing around each other, their clenched fists hitting the air. Every now and then Ferro would throw a quick side glance at an open window facing in the direction of Brusò as he went on saying, "I've understood you better than anybody else, Rodolfo, I am with you. Always been. Last night, the act, the event, was ripening; now this is the morning, today is yesterday's tomorrow, the hour has struck, here we are, this is the moment. On guard, Crocetti Vidal! I'm doing this for your own good. It isn't because you automatically voted against me in censorship committees or because you provided Benn with damaging information that was likely to send me to prison—no, Crocetti Vidal, this is mainly for your own good."

Now the hand-to-hand fight began. After the first hard blows Ferro's voice resumed, punctuated by the dull sound of the thumps: "You're strong, you swing at me pretty hard too, but it's all right, it's worthwhile, for your own good. This is your own morning, Benito Giuseppe, this particular tomorrow is all yours; now I know why Rodolfo Spada told me last night to come here: to present you with this sudden morning, all yours."

He was stopped by a direct hit in his teeth; he reacted by plunging with mad fury on Crocetti Vidal, grabbing his cheeks, hitting, slapping, manipulating, as though he wanted to remodel the man's face. Both moaned as if between pain and pleasure.

At last Crocetti Vidal wriggled himself free and stood isolated, leaving his face uncovered, out in the open—a new face, glowing, its enormous green eyes now naked, freed from the thick glass of the lenses, cleared in their full glory.

Matilde says that at that vision her heart trembled with tenderness while she felt her eyes moistening with tears of compassion and joy.

Angelantonio commanded soberly, "Now you stop," and his words were immediately followed by stillness and silence broken only by the heavy panting of the two men.

B. G. Crocetti Vidal's head was the most important object in that room, in that village, in the whole countryside, perhaps in the whole of Venetian nature—a head shiny as a brass ball, and at the same time juicy as a ripe fruit; from open scratches issued the blood.

Fornasier advanced and placed a hand on Ferro's shoulder, whispering, "Now I'll take you to be repaired," while he signaled to Matilde at the other end of the room: "Dear, you've never wanted me; perhaps this was the reason; now I'll leave him with you."

Crocetti Vidal staggered toward Matilde's open arms; she supported him on the way to the bedroom.

Here she settled him on the bed; she brought cotton and hot water from the bathroom, and stretched out beside him, she sponged the wounds and washed his face. Then he looked at her with immeasureably deep eyes, green lighthouse beacons liquefied in a fog; he stammered, "You drink my blood."

It was the first time in his life that after having uttered a sentence, he was aware of not understanding what he had said. It would have been impossible for him to decide whether his "You drink" was indicative or imperative, an observation or an invitation. Thus the speech which had sustained him up to that hour in his life fell apart; and Crocetti Vidal ventured into the immense and craggy world of human talk.

From unfathomed depths, disconnected phrases emerged while Matilde was leading him to the completion of love: "I am alive. I am the truth. Liberation movements. I liberate you, Mother."

It was reconstructed later, at the hospital, that after a first act of copulation with Matilde, the initial one in his life, Crocetti Vidal went through abundant attacks of vomiting.

Then, according to his own testimony, given in the style of free association, he thought of going directly from the bathroom to an operating room to have his testicles amputated. He felt intoxicated by the very thought. Meanwhile, he declared, after vomiting he had a feeling of liberation, euphoria.

He went back to Matilde and fell asleep. He snored for about one hour. In his sleep he mumbled again, "You drink my blood."

Caressing his forehead, Matilde murmured unheard, "No, I do not drink your blood. If anything, I lick your wounds, and then, in a beautiful hospital, I'll always be close to you."

Between dreaming and awaking he spoke with a limpid voice: "I feel well. No, no surgery. I am in a tunnel of flowers! The garden near our school! The school bell at noon! Speak to me, Celotti; I never told you that I only pretended I wasn't listening to you, but I always did, I listened to your words, every one of them, Celotti!"

Celotti, Adelmo. The boy sitting next to him in class. It was noon, like now, and the young teacher, Signorina Apicetta, was saying from her desk, "Class, don't you ever forget it: poetry, fundamentally, is metaphor."

Beside him, Celotti started whispering for the thousandth time, tenderly, ecstatically, "How I would like to make her, that big cow. Look at her knees, her thighs. She magnetizes me. She makes me feel exalted. Notice that I am dying with hunger, but if you should tell me to choose between a beautiful plate of rigatoni with meat sauce and dying in a state of exaltation with that big cow, I'd choose dying. Beautiful, sublime, blazing . . ."

The bell tolls twelve in the sky.

". . . blazing in the noon sky."

Here too the bell strikes noon, and completely awakened, Peppino sees himself joined to his only teacher, Matilde, entwined with her, received, contained in her. At last he recognizes her, whole, open.

"Oh!" A sharp, happy cry; then biting, tongue clacking, and on that vast Venetian bed a total tumult.

He could see his own cries spreading out over the fields, over the villages with clock towers and poplar trees standing straight in the noon air, and on and on, to the sandbanks, to the waters and the beautiful islands, sunlit, saved. The whole world was goodness, and all of it was Matilde; his high sonorous voice invoked it all, praised it all in her.

"My joy, my bovine beloved, my wide-thighed, celestial, magnetizing teacher, blazing banner, sublime metaphor, my own, my own, big angelic cow, here I am, I come, I fly, I laugh, I sing, I die, thank you."

Venice and Beverly Hills, 1968–1971

ABOUT THE AUTHOR

P. M. Pasinetti was born and grew up in Venice. In 1935–37 he came to study in the United States, where his first published fiction appeared in *The Southern Review*. Mr. Pasinetti has since contributed to various literary reviews in this country, and since the age of eighteen has written pieces for magazines and newspapers in Italy, where he has also done occasional work on screenplays. His first book, three novelettes, was published by Mondadori in 1942.

Mr. Pasinetti first thought of teaching as a means of moving from his native country. After lectureships at Göttingen and Stockholm (where he spent most of the war years) he returned to the United States in 1946, taught briefly at Bennington and received a doctorate at Yale. He has since been associated with U.C.L.A., where he holds a professorship. He was appointed to the university's Institute for Creative Arts for 1964–65, and in 1965 received an award from the National Institute of Arts and Letters with a citation for fiction written in "the grand style of tradition but with a probing modern imagination." His first three novels, *Venetian Red* (1960), *The Smile on the Face of the Lion* (1965) and *From the Academy Bridge* (1970), were enthusiastically praised by critics both in this country and in Europe.